To: Ken

Verne R. Albright

HATRED IS AN ACID
An Unforgettable Novel about the Black Experience in America
Verne R. Albright

For more information email: albrightv@shaw.ca

ISBN: 978-1-62660-174-1

Book and cover design: Michael Campbell, MC Writing Services

Front cover illustration: *The Death of Crispus Attucks,* one of roughly 5,000 African Americans to fight against the British during the American Revolutionary War. Engraving by Paul Revere.

Back cover photos from the National Archive and Library of Congress. By the end of the American Civil War in 1865, an estimated 180,000 Black men had made up about ten percent of the victorious Union Army. Of these, forty thousand were killed and twenty-six were awarded Medals of Honor for bravery.

Other Best-Selling Novels By Verne R. Albright

Playing Chess with God

2019 Online Book Club's "Book of the Year." Best Seller.

The Wrath of God

A Best Seller with almost all 5-star reviews.

Horseback Across Three Americas

Winner of the 2021 Best "Equine Journey" Literary Award at EQUUS Television's EQUUS Film and Arts Festival!

Discovering Her Worth: A Woman in a Man's World

Best Seller. All 5-star reviews.

Available now at Amazon.com

HATRED
is an
ACID

An Unforgettable Novel about the Black Experience in America

Dedicated to my incomparable editor and test reader Sherla Alberola, and to Mimi Busk-Downey, who—over the years—has helped me in many ways.

Contents

CHAPTER ONE
HUNS AND VANDALS

NEWS ANCHORMAN Brian Waterman stood in front of a television camera, holding a microphone in his free hand. Behind him, a battle-ready California National Guard armored personnel carrier was outlined against a Los Angeles neighborhood in flames.

Waterman's other arm was cradled in an improvised sling. A ban on live T.V. coverage meant his comments would be broadcast later. This allowed him to start again, coming at the story from another angle.

He desperately wanted viewers to understand the violence convulsing America's second-largest city. To explain, however, he needed to understand. Unfortunately, he didn't.

"Tonight," he started again, "hatred festering in Los Angeles' South Central district is driving residents to destroy the very neighborhoods where they live and work."

Covering stories in the past, he'd observed that cameras usually brought out people's best behavior.

Tonight, however, the first man he'd interviewed had screamed, "You fucking White newsmen portray us Blacks as subhuman."

With cameraman Dale Praiss recording his every action, the man aimed a shotgun at Waterman and fidgeted with its safety for a terrifying moment, then walked away looking back across his shoulder, eyes blazing with contempt.

Moments later, Waterman and his cameraman were knocked down by a mob stampeding toward the latest looting. They followed and filmed a group stealing from an electronics store. There a man with a crowbar smashed the camera, then broke Waterman's wrist.

With his good hand, he drove KTLA's van and back-up camera to an area protected by National Guard troops. There he offered commentary while Praiss selected camera angles with soldiers, armored personnel carriers, burning buildings, and looters in the background.

A desperate-sounding voice burst from Waterman's Los Angeles Police Department scanner.

"We're under fire at Florence and Normandie. We need reinforcements fast."

"Let's go," Waterman said to his cameraman. "That should give us some great shots."

Waterman's wrist throbbed as he sped through deserted streets, past burning buildings and vehicles. Another transmission crackled from the scanner. It was from the pilot of a police helicopter hovering above Florence and Normandie.

"We have to leave," a frantic voice said. "They're shooting at us. If those officers don't get help soon, their wives will be widows and their children orphans."

Its blade making a whump, whump sound, the copter passed overhead.

Waterman made a U-turn, shifted into reverse and continued on, looking over his shoulder. Backing around a corner onto a deserted street, he saw policemen hunkered behind their cars, then parked KTLA's refrigerator-white van in the shadows.

Hastily, Praiss set up the spare camera, switched to the telephoto lens, and peered through the viewfinder. What he saw was an enraged woman, her body rigid with tension, urging the crowd on. He centered her in the viewfinder and started recording.

"I can get close enough to pick up what she's saying," Waterman whispered, as he grabbed a wireless directional microphone.

"We've taken too many risks tonight," Praiss said. "What that lady is saying won't be suitable for prime time. We've got some great footage. Let's get out of here."

"Go ahead," Waterman said, "but leave the camera and van for me."

"Good luck." Praiss hurried away on foot.

Waterman filmed the mob until a group started toward him. They were no more than twenty feet away when they froze, startled by the roar of diesel engines.

Broken glass vibrated from nearby window frames and shattered on the sidewalk as two National Guard armored personnel carriers came around a corner and sped past. The street shook beneath Waterman's feet. When the viewfinder showed APC's and rioters at the same time, he turned on the camera.

Politicians on both sides would twist this confrontation to fit their agendas. He wanted his viewers to see it firsthand.

—◦—

In the mob at the intersection, Muhammad Nasheed's followers spread out and continued to goad the rioters. They were Muslims and Black, but they weren't Black Muslims. They were real Muslims who paid allegiance to the Prophet

Muhammad and yearned to live in their own territory, independent of White America.

Black Muslims had once wanted the same. In the mid-1960s, the Nation of Islam's leader, Louis Farrakhan, had said: "Since we cannot get along with Whites in peace and equality, we believe our contributions to this land and the suffering forced upon us by White America justifies our demand for complete separation in a state or territory of our own."

Thirty years later Farrakhan announced that if Blacks could get freedom, justice, and equal rights within the political, economic, and social system of America, there would be no need for a separate Black state.

But Allah had revealed to Muhammad Nasheed—namesake of the prophet Muhammad—that He wanted Muslims to govern the world and would help them achieve that goal.

Most of Nasheed's followers had once been Christians with slave names. Now they believed in the Koran and—like Cassius Clay and Lew Alcindor, who'd become Muhammad Ali and Kareem Abdul-Jabber—they had Muslim names.

They'd sworn that America's next racial flare-up would fulfill the prediction made by Lord Thomas Macaulay, a British historian, in 1857.

Appalled by America's treatment of its Black slaves, Macaulay had warned: "Your republic will be as fearfully plundered and laid waste by barbarians in the twentieth century as the Roman Empire was in the fifth, with this difference: the Huns and Vandals who ravaged the Roman Empire came from without and your Huns and Vandals will have been engendered within your own country, by your own institutions."

But there had been no twentieth century race war. Nasheed had dedicated his life to making Macaulay's prediction come true. Better late than never, the time had come.

CHAPTER TWO
THE TOURIST MURDERS

THAT YEAR, Los Angeles had been on track to draw fifty million visitors who'd spend some forty billion dollars. But the murders of White tourists had people vacationing elsewhere.

The L.A. Convention and Visitors Bureau had tried to limit the damage to the local economy by warning travelers to avoid South Central. That area, however, is bigger than Manhattan, has a larger population than San Francisco, and is difficult to recognize or avoid.

After searching for hours, a German newsman had asked the police for directions and discovered he'd been there all day.

In other American ghettos, the majority live in multi-family units. In South Central, most live in small houses with porches and yards. There are parks, playgrounds, and wide, palm-tree-lined streets. Set apart from commercial districts, residential areas have less traffic, litter, and noise than other inner cities.

Every night for weeks, people in Los Angeles had switched on the television news to find out how many tourists were murdered that day. That number was declining. However, thousands objected to the Convention and Visitors Bureau's warnings for tourists to avoid South Central.

In response the Bureau had stopped handing out maps and toned down its warnings. This concession puzzled

California's Lieutenant Governor, Larry Winslow. The victims had all been Caucasian. The murders were clearly intended to provoke racial unrest. Why not warn outsiders about the risks involved in going there?

Larry had been a successful fifty-seven-year-old businessman when he allowed himself to be drafted as the Republican candidate for Lieutenant Governor. The campaign had been exhilarating, but serving had been boring.

Elected separately, California's Governor and Lieutenant Governor sometimes came from opposing political parties. Governor Robert Webster, a Democrat, had kept Larry, a Republican, out of public view.

Governor Webster's administrative assistant had summoned Larry that morning. Six feet tall, slender and fit with pewter-gray hair and intense blue eyes, he left his office and hurried across Sacramento's Capitol Park, without his bodyguard.

Inside California's Capitol Building Larry saw a handsome, middle-aged Black man standing below the rotunda's stained glass dome. Seeing his distinctive blue Crips bandanna, people gave him a wide berth.

The Crips—largest Black gang in Los Angeles—had controlled South Central's narcotics trade until rival gangs united to form the Bloods, whose bandannas were red. Subsequently, the two gangs had fought a forty-year drug war that snuffed out at least seventeen thousand lives.

"Long time since I saw a Crips bandanna," Larry said, stopping beside the man.

"No one wears gang insignia these days," the man replied. "They help police and rival gang members identify you. I figured mine might help me get the Governor's attention so I can tell him what's happening in South Central."

His voice echoed under the rotunda's domed ceiling. Periodically, a tic contorted his face, pulling one side of his mouth higher than the other.

"I'm the Lieutenant Governor," Larry said. "You can tell me."

"Someone's uniting the Crips and Bloods," the man continued, "so they can fight the police instead of each other. I used to be a Crip. Since I left, I've worked non-stop to get kids out of both gangs and—"

"We've had a complaint," one of two police officers interrupted. "According to Governor Webster's receptionist, you tried to force your way into his private office."

"I have important news for him," the man said, agitated.

"What's your name?"

"Wade Hardin."

"Don't make us arrest you, Mr. Hardin."

"Arrest me!" Hardin's tic became more conspicuous. "For what?"

"Disturbing the peace. The Governor's receptionist intends to file a complaint unless you leave the building now."

"Not until I talk to the Governor," Hardin shouted stubbornly.

"In that case, Sir, you're under arrest."

The officer and his partner escorted Hardin outside. Larry walked to the annex and into an office behind oversize double doors framed by black and gold Montana marble. Instead of sending him to the waiting area as usual, the receptionist ushered him to Governor Webster's office.

Webster, who sat behind his desk, had olive skin, expensively barbered black hair—combed straight back—and an engaging Dennis Quaid smile. Seeing Larry, he put out his cigar and waved his arms to disperse the smoke.

They shook hands, and Webster gestured to a chair on the other side of his desk.

"As you know," he said when they were seated, "these Tourist Murders are costing Southern California's economy billions of dollars. Worse yet, a recent study by RAND Corporation has concluded that South Central is ripe for the worst riot in American history."

"I just spoke with a man in the rotunda," Larry said. "He claimed to have information you should hear. It supports RAND Corporation's report."

"Hell, he just tried to force his way into my office. He's a fruit cake." Webster circled his index finger near his temple. "I've appointed a bipartisan Race Relations Commission. I want you to chair it."

"I have no expertise on that subject."

"You have a reputation for getting jobs done," the Governor replied. "The Commission's members are politicians and intellectuals who'll need someone to keep them focused. I'm also going to ask your wife to advise them. Emily knows race relations as well as anyone in America."

"I'll give you my answer tomorrow morning," Larry said.

"Be here by 9:00 AM. I'll introduce you to the Commission before you give your final answer." Webster stood and balanced a loose-leaf binder on one palm as if weighing it. "This is RAND Corporation's report. It's top secret. Keep it under wraps."

As Larry walked back to his office, his mother came to mind. She'd passionately believed racism was evil, and his values had come from her. After quitting college, he'd become a policeman, full of goodwill and determined to make a difference.

—~~—

During a robbery when he was thirteen, Muhammad Nasheed had shot an uncooperative Korean store owner in front of a security camera. Then, unrecognizable in a ski mask, he'd followed a wire from the camera to a recorder in another room and stolen the video tape. Countless times since then, he'd watched his bullet blow off a chunk of his victim's skull.

Later Nasheed had converted to Islam and studied at Iran's Tehran University. There Muslim fundamentalists invited him to their madrasa, a school where young Muslims were prepared for Holy War.

Back home, he'd opened a madrasa in South Central, operated by an English-speaking Saudi imam.

He'd found allies among the battle-hardened Crips and Bloods, who'd fought the longest war in U.S. history. In forty years, seventeen thousand had been killed. After years of getting better, the situation was now worsening.

Both gangs were divided into subgroups called sets. Nasheed befriended leaders who had impressed him and paid them more than their set earned selling illegal drugs. That money came from Iran's Islamic fundamentalists and was only a fraction of what they spent opposing the Great Satan, the United States.

In return, those leaders pulled their supporters out of the drug wars and joined Nasheed's Holy War. For months, soldiers sent by Iran's Revolutionary Guard had been training Nasheed's men to use modern Russian weapons.

CHAPTER THREE
AMERICA'S MOST INTRACTABLE PROBLEM

LARRY'S AIDES would disagree with each other on whether he should accept the Governor's offer. Though sometimes frustrating, their contradictory advice was always useful. This time, it would be especially so. Ted Roffman was White and Michael Bridges was Black.

Roffman's Irish blood showed in his craggy face and unruly eyebrows. His opinions were rigid, his manner abrasive, and his language colorful. He had once described Governor Webster as, "similar to a drunk who uses lamp posts for support rather than illumination."

Bridges was a tall liberal with chiseled features and gentle eyes that made people trust him and want him to trust them. He politely stood his ground when he and Roffman disagreed. He'd been approached to run for office, and Larry had been fortunate to get him.

By 3:00 PM Larry was in his office, sitting in the high-backed chair behind his desk. His aides listened as he revealed the Governor's offer.

As usual, Roffman responded first.

"Webster wants you to be a lightning rod for the inevitable criticism," he grumped. "He'll make you responsible for the job, but won't give you the authority you need to do it."

"It will also give me an opportunity," Larry offered, "to recommend some changes in Blacks' behavior, something that's rarely done these days."

"That will be tricky," Bridges said. "As I see it, a chairman's job is to lead discussions, make sure everyone's heard, and keep the proceedings focused. To do this, he or she must be perceived as impartial."

Larry handed each of his aides a list of the Commission's members.

Glancing at his, Roffman offered, "Top heavy with liberal activists. They'll automatically pander to Blacks by blaming their failings on Whites."

"The only dyed-in-the-wool radical is Avery King," Bridges declared. "The others are open minded."

"Am I qualified for the job?" Larry asked.

"Abundantly," Bridges said. "Your biggest responsibility will be organizing the Commission and keeping it focused. You're exceptionally good at that. To prepare yourself, I recommend reading *A Nation's Destiny,* a book by Lewis Franklin."

"Can you please get me a copy?"

"With pleasure," Bridges offered. "Shall I also get copies of the best studies done after the Watts and Rodney King Riots?"

"Those are the last thing you need," Roffman protested. "No reputable psychiatrist tells patients that all their problems are other people's fault. But that's what this Commission will wind up doing if it dusts off tired old studies and regurgitates them."

"One more thing," Larry said. "I'd like each of you to make a list of South Central's most serious problems and people who've offered fresh solutions."

As Larry's aides left, Bridge's gait was smooth and athletic. Roffman dragged his feet. He appeared to be sulking but wasn't. That was how he always walked.

Both his assistants were priceless assets, and occupying the middle ground between them had kept Larry afloat in the unfamiliar world of politics.

—m—

Larry's high school class in Fallon, Nevada, had one Negro, as they were called in those days. Larry had never known Andrew Biggs. In Larry's senior year, he and his classmates had elected Biggs class president to compensate for the racism they assumed he'd suffered.

They didn't, however, befriend him, which Larry later realized would have been far more meaningful.

That had been Larry's second experience with a Negro. The first was when he was eight. He and his mom were going home after visiting her mother in Alabama. He was fascinated by a Black man in a Coast Guard uniform at the back of the bus. Before the trip began, the driver closed a curtain that separated Negroes from Whites.

After they left the Deep South, that curtain was left open, and Larry sat next to the coast guardsman. After talking for hours, he and Sammy Lewis exchanged addresses.

A month later, Larry received a letter in which Lewis described a dramatic coast guard rescue at sea. Larry replied and Lewis wrote again.

Larry's regret for not answering that letter was sharpened while he and his mother followed Martin Luther King's civil rights movement on television. He could still picture the Negro demonstrators, men in suits and women in Sunday go-to-meeting dresses.

He'd silently cheered as King answered smug White supremacists' vile insults with calm logic. He'd also felt shame when a White jury acquitted the men responsible for murdering a Black and two White civil rights workers in Mississippi.

—∞—

When Larry saw no use for what he was learning at the University of California, Los Angeles, he became a policeman, like his father before him. When assigned to Watts, part of the area later known as South Central, he accepted.

Most Blacks he met while doing that job were very different from those he'd seen on television in the Civil Rights era. He was unprepared for the violence that seethed beneath Watts' surface.

He couldn't believe how often residents shot or knifed each other... how frequently men abandoned their children or beat their wives... the indifference to suffering... the drinking, drugs, and profanity... the way people squandered money when they had it.

"Real life niggers are nothing like you've been taught," his partner told him during his first day on the job. Slowly he stopped idolizing Negroes and became disappointed in them.

His idealism gone, Larry still took no pleasure from the insults, petty cruelties, and humiliations the other Los Angeles Police Department officers inflicted on people in Watts.

"There must be a lot of Negroes in jail for things they didn't do," he'd told his partner one night.

"So what?" his partner had sneered. "If they didn't commit that particular crime, they did something else."

For two years, Larry stayed with LAPD, treating Negroes with courtesy and stepping in when fellow officers were harsh. He also made himself unpopular by putting only the truth in his arrest reports, even when other officers pressured him to embellish these with details that would help the District Attorney get convictions.

Soon after leaving LAPD, he discovered his genius for business and founded an import-export empire.

After eighteen years of his personal attention, his companies practically ran themselves. He was looking for a new challenge when friends convinced him to run for Lieutenant Governor, as a stepping stone to becoming Governor or a U.S. Senator.

Now, thirty-four years after Larry turned his back on America's most intractable problem, Governor Webster had offered him an opportunity to try again. He liked the idea of working with his wife and was tempted.

When Larry met Emily, she was teaching race relations at the University of Chicago. After he hired several Blacks—who were subsequently treated badly by his other employees—the company's human relations manager tried to fire the Blacks.

Larry fired him instead and on the recommendation of his replacement, he called Emily. She was a respected expert on Black/White relations. Her advice had been helpful so he'd called for more.

Back then, he lived in San Francisco and she in Chicago. They liked each other immediately, and after their business dealings were over, the phone calls continued. When Larry traveled to San Antonio, Texas, on business, Emily flew in and knocked on his room's door.

"You don't look anything like I imagined," she said when he opened the door.

Recognizing her voice, he asked, "Is that good or bad?"

"Good," she replied. "I didn't expect someone with your intelligence and decency to be nice-looking as well. That seemed like too much to hope for."

"Is that why you didn't ask for a photograph?" he teased.

"I didn't need one. I liked you, and didn't care how you look."

She had been exotically beautiful, and of mixed race, being the daughter of a plantation owner and a former household slave who had gained her freedom after years of running his household.

"Have you had dinner yet?" he asked.

They strolled to San Antonio's delightful River Walk and ate at Biga on the Banks Restaurant. Afterward, they sat on a bench under a willow tree, talking until the sun came up.

By the time they said good-bye at the airport a week later, their courtship was underway. At forty-one, Larry had never married and was still waiting for the right woman to come along.

Emily's age—she was twelve years younger—had concerned him only briefly. The only other uncomfortable moment came after she revealed she'd had an affair with a Black man. Larry hadn't expected an attractive woman her age to be a virgin. But somehow that news had made him uncomfortable, probably because it exposed a prejudice of which he'd been blissfully unaware.

At their wedding reception, his mother had memorably told him, "I'd wish you good luck, but you won't need it. Emily's as special as you are."

At first, others had looked at them with envy and approval. Over time, however, they'd drifted apart—not due to the presence of bad times as much as the absence of good ones. Now their relationship was best described as one that had fallen short of its potential.

CHAPTER FOUR
AS IF TOMORROW WASN'T THERE

AFTER ROFFMAN and Bridges went home, Larry and Don Maxwell, his bodyguard, took the elevator to underground parking. Uncomfortable having a man open doors for him, tell him where to sit and stand, and check rooms before he went in, Larry was still adjusting to his protector.

While gridlocked in the nightly traffic jam, Larry decided to accept Governor Webster's offer. He hoped Emily would, as well. Working together could draw them closer.

After a long commute, Maxwell turned into a driveway with a stone wall on one side and a line of daffodil clumps on the other. Using a remote control he opened one of three overhead doors on a garage attached to a two-story, steep-roofed Tudor house with a patterned brick façade between dark timbers.

After Larry got out, Maxwell waited for the door to close and latch before driving away.

Larry let himself into the house and hurried to Emily's office. She wasn't there. His eyes were drawn to the poster-size photograph on the wall behind her desk.

Taken by a newsman during the Watts riot, it showed a pregnant Black lady and a policeman glaring at each other. For Emily, it symbolized America's racial divide.

The officer—exhausted and staring at the woman's protruding belly—seemed to disapprove of her bringing another of *them* into the world. The woman looked outraged because he'd decided who her baby would be before it was even born.

"Hi." Emily's voice came from the hallway's far end.

Today was her birthday. She wore the outfit he'd given her that morning. As she walked toward him, the softly draped fabric of her skirt swirled around long, slender legs.

Abruptly she interrupted her bouncy walk and did a fashion model pirouette for his approval.

Larry was reminded of how very much he'd once loved her. Back then, few would have guessed he was twelve years older, but yesterday a stranger had assumed he was her father.

"You made a good choice," Emily said. "I've gotten many compliments on how nice I look in this outfit."

"It would be more accurate to say how nice that outfit looks on you," Larry said, eyes focused on the tight, short-sleeved, cream-colored, pullover sweater that emphasized the firm curves of a younger woman.

"How'd things go at New Beginnings?" Larry asked.

They'd chosen that Adoption Agency because it imposed no age limit as long as both adopting parents were in good health.

"Today they told me about the biological mother," she said. "She's a lot like me—younger of course, but with a similar I.Q., level of success, and physical appearance. The baby should be a good fit."

Emily had been thirty-five when they'd married. A year later, a doctor told her she'd never have children. That same day they'd begun their effort to adopt. After a three-year wait, they were scheduled to receive a baby girl any day now.

"I haven't been this happy for a long time." Emily ran her long fingers through her sandy-brown hair, looking at him through pale gray-blue eyes.

She didn't know he'd been responsible for their long wait. He hadn't known that himself until he'd asked New Beginnings' director why two babies had gone to people who applied after they had.

"The interviewer said you were unusually specific in describing the background from which you want your baby to come," the director had explained, "and we haven't yet found what you want."

"How'd *your* day go?" Emily asked.

"The RAND Corporation is predicting another riot in South Central," Larry replied. "Governor Webster appointed a Commission to recommend ways of averting it. He asked me to be the chairman, and he wants you to advise us."

"Sounds like the kind of challenge you enjoy," she said. "Did you accept?"

"I will if you will," he replied.

"With a new baby, I won't have time."

Emily had taken a one-year leave of absence from teaching at California State University's Sacramento campus and was currently furnishing and decorating a nursery beside their bedroom.

"Advising the Commission won't take much time," Larry said. "You can do most of it from home. You don't seem to like the idea of our working together?"

"You won't like my answer."

"I'd like to hear it."

"You're not the right person for this job," she said after a long silence. "You'd never do or say anything unkind to a Black person, but you judge them as a group—not as individuals."

The words stung but didn't surprise him. Lately they'd found it difficult to discuss race. What she saw as truth, he saw as wishful thinking. What he saw as being realistic, she saw as prejudice.

Talking had also been difficult early in their relationship, but for a different reason. After their week in San Antonio, they'd returned to their respective homes and begun an initially unsatisfying long-distance courtship.

Emily spent her waking hours at work and couldn't make or receive personal calls on University of Chicago phones.

"I can't afford a cellular phone," she said when Larry suggested she get one. "Besides, figuring them out is beyond me."

The next day, Federal Express delivered an amazingly simple cell phone. Larry had prepaid a year's service. All she had to do to call him was press the automatic dialing button.

There had never been a successful slave revolt in North America, but in the late 1700s, a hundred thousand African slaves had ravaged the Caribbean island of Haiti. Led by Toussaint L'Ouverture, they set fire to hundreds of sugar, coffee, cocoa, cotton, and indigo plantations.

"We swear to destroy the Whites and all they possess," was the slaves' battle cry. "Let us die rather than fail to keep this vow."

During their rebellion's first days, Haiti's slaves slaughtered four thousand of their White oppressors, often with little more than bare hands and farm implements.

A rain of embers drove all ships from Port-Au-Prince's harbor. For weeks, flames brightened the night and smoke

darkened the day to where there was little difference. Haiti's bright glow could be seen from Cuba.

Next Toussaint organized an army that took control of Haiti, abolished slavery, and invaded the neighboring Dominican Republic to free slaves there. He'd once won seven battles in seven days and was reportedly wounded in action many times.

Later his men defeated British and Spanish troops, then inflicted the first defeat suffered by Napoleon's Grande Armée. At the height of his power, Toussaint gave orders to 55,000 men. By comparison, George Washington never commanded more than twenty thousand.

American plantation owners were terrified that Toussaint's soldiers would land on the Gulf Coast and start an uprising that would dwarf those in Haiti and the Dominican Republic.

After referring to Toussaint's soldiers as cannibals, Thomas Jefferson urged Congress to abolish trade and cut off communication with Haiti and the Dominican Republic to keep word of the revolt from inspiring America's slaves.

With the modern weapons his army would soon receive, Muhammad Nasheed was confident that his would be a far more astonishing success.

CHAPTER FIVE
REVOLUTIONARIES OR HOODLUMS?

WITH RARE exceptions, Larry went to bed at 10:00 PM, got up at 3:00 AM, and then read for four interruption-free hours. He'd done this all his adult life, and calculated that sleeping only five hours gave him an extra forty-six productive days every year.

Recent research, however, had shown that people who slept five or less hours suffered from Short Sleep Syndrome. This misled them into believing they were functioning well when they were in fact less mentally efficient and suffered more chronic diseases than people who slept at least seven hours.

Larry, however, always awoke refreshed. Evidently, he had the rare gene that allows some people to function normally on 5 hours sleep, a group so small it's statistically zero.

By the time Don Maxwell picked Larry up the following morning, he'd digested the RAND Corporation's report.

At 9:00 AM in Governor Webster's office, Larry accepted his appointment.

"Good," Webster said. "I'm leaving on a trade mission to Asia this afternoon. My assistant, Rita Moore, will introduce you to the Commission's members."

Larry had read their resumes. The six from the State Legislature favored enlarging existing programs. The two from the private sector believed Blacks' lives would improve when their behavior changed. The two State Senators would monitor opinion polls before deciding.

Larry's last introduction was to Avery King, the best-known person there. Black, he'd served in the State Assembly for thirty years. *Time* Magazine had called his aggressive in-your-face demeanor: 'more suited to a wrestler than a public servant.'

"What are your qualifications for this job?" King demanded after shaking Larry's hand.

"I'll pass out my resume," Larry replied, "after today's meeting."

King held out his hand, palm up and said, "I may ask for a vote of confidence in you—or no confidence, depending on your qualifications. I want to see that list now."

"It's my policy," Larry replied, "to pass out printed material after meetings so it won't be distracting."

King joined the Commission's other members at the glossy, oak conference table.

"We've got an uphill fight," Roffman whispered to Larry when they were alone. "Next year, most of these folks will stand for reelection in Black districts. They won't allow this report to even suggest that Blacks share any blame whatsoever."

"Webster didn't mention there'd be a meeting today," Larry said quietly. "I'm not prepared."

"The bastard sent you into a minefield without a map. He fears you'll run against him in the next election and if this committee fails, he'll use you as a whipping boy."

"Why do you suppose he appointed a hothead like King?"

"King has represented South Central in the California Assembly for years," Ted replied. "The residents will take this report more seriously if he's among its authors."

Roffman and Bridges sat near the court reporter, who was unpacking her stenographic machine to keep a transcript of the proceedings. From the podium Larry called the meeting to order. The Commission's members faced him. Four were Black, four Hispanic, and four Caucasian.

"I have no expertise in race relations," Larry began. "I'm here because I have a reputation as an organizer. I can also offer a unique perspective because I was once a police officer in South Central and saw examples of the police brutality that threatens to provoke a third riot there.

"Our Commission will waste an opportunity if it proposes more programs like those that have failed. Our job is not to assign blame. At times, however, we must do that before we can suggest workable solutions.

"Where Whites need to change their behavior, we must clearly say so. If Blacks need to make adjustments, we must point that out, despite our sympathy for their centuries of suffering."

When Larry paused, uncertain of how to proceed, Michael Bridges handed him a note. He read it and looked up.

"Today's speaker," he announced, "is Winston Baker, a member of the team that wrote the RAND Corporation's report."

Baker shyly walked to the podium and Larry adjusted the microphone down to his height.

"I'm not a sociologist," Baker began quietly. "My specialty is psychiatry, specifically the study of hatred. When we became aware of the mood in South Central, I collected psychological profiles there and was astonished by the anger and hatred."

He droned on in a voice with little inflection, boring his listeners until he finally said something not in his report.

"In all of Mexico, only the capital has more Mexicans than Los Angeles. Right now—largely because Blacks and African-Americans compete for jobs—Hispanics will most likely sit on the sidelines if there's another riot. During the Rodney King riot, Hispanics were a third of those killed and half of those arrested. They've made significant progress since then—especially in the area of employment—and have comparatively little to protest."

—∞—

When Larry returned to the lectern, Horace Grayson, a Black Ph.D., raised his hand.

"Yes, Doctor Grayson," Larry said.

Elegant and serene, Grayson stood and looked from face to face all the way around the table.

"Before a riot," he said, "people's passions must be inflamed. Such a process is underway in South Central because of the Walter Jezierski trial." Looking at Larry, he added, "Having been a policeman, you must have an interesting perspective."

Jezierski was a Los Angeles county deputy sheriff, on trial for fatally shooting an unarmed fifteen-year-old Black boy while arresting him. Larry didn't know the details behind the headlines.

He turned to Michael Bridges and said, "Put that on Friday's agenda. That will give everyone time to prepare for a fruitful discussion."

"If you're not familiar with that case, Mr. Winslow," Avery King boomed, "you're the only person here who isn't. Few Whites care about Jezierski's victim any more than they worry about the thousands of African-Americans who've died in our city's drug wars. Not until White tourists were murdered did your constituents finally demand that something be done about the gangs."

"Add the gangs to Friday's agenda," Larry told Bridges.

"I object," Grayson continued calmly, "to calling the event we hope to prevent a riot. That word suggests violence devoid of social meaning. It will be more accurate if our report refers to the possibility of a *rebellion* or *uprising*."

King jumped up and bellowed, "For a century after the Civil War, Whites rioted in Black neighborhoods. For no reason they burned, bombed, looted, and murdered. The authorities did nothing.

"But when Blacks protest in response to monstrous injustices—they're labeled inherently violent. Hell, White riots gave Blacks the idea for that tactic.

"Today, riot is synonymous with Black riot, but the so-called Watts and Rodney King Riots were clearly rebellions. That's why participants burned businesses owned by the oppressors but didn't touch residences, schools, churches, libraries, public buildings, or Black-owned businesses."

When no one presented the argument's other side, Larry asked, "Were looters who targeted liquor stores and shops full of expensive merchandise making a socially relevant point or simply stealing?"

"Sometimes," King interrupted, raising his voice in an attempt to drown Larry out, "violence is the only way to—"

"Gentlemen," the court reporter snapped. "I can't keep an accurate transcript if two people talk at the same time."

"In future discussions," Larry said, "we need to offer more than our opinions. We should document our statements."

"I'd like to read two pertinent quotations into the record of today's meeting," King said, opening a book. "The first comes from French political scientist Alexis de Tocqueville.

"He wrote: 'If ever America undergoes great revolutions, they will be brought about by the presence of the Black race on American soil, and will have been caused by the inequality of condition.'"

"The other is attributed to the Marquis de Lafayette, a French military officer who served in George Washington's Continental Army during the American Revolution. He also arranged for France to supply America with materiel, loans, advisors, troops, and naval support.

After that revolution succeeded, however, he wrote, 'I would have never drawn my sword in the cause of America, if I could have conceived that thereby I was helping to found a land of slavery.'"

"Has anything changed," Larry asked, "since he wrote those noble words?"

"Everything," Dolores Menke, a White business owner, volunteered. "We've had a Civil War, the Emancipation Proclamation, and affirmative action, as well as countless new laws and groundbreaking Supreme Court decisions."

"A suggestion," Larry said. "At our upcoming meetings why don't we invite experts from various sides of the race debate, with special emphasis on those who favor untried solutions."

After adjourning the meeting, Larry met with King in the Governor's office.

"Can we find a way to work together in harmony?" he asked.

"How?" King replied. "We don't seem to agree on anything."

"We have a similar taste in tie pins," Larry said, probing to see if King had a sense of humor. "I used to import tie pins exactly like yours. Where'd you get it?"

"My son brought it from Persia," King told him.

"You're referring to Iran?"

"That's its modern name, yes."

"What was your son doing there?"

"Attending the University of Tehran," King said, "and if you're wondering why I sent him to be educated by one of America's sworn enemies, I didn't. That decision was his."

On the drive back to Larry's office, Ted Roffman told Larry, "You did an impressive job of keeping Avery King from taking control of the meeting."

"In the process," Larry replied, "I violated the unspoken rule that requires a chairman to be impartial. I fear that may have alienated several committee members. Delores Menke was the only person who took my side today."

—m—

Muhammad Nasheed had bribed a courier and gotten a copy of the RAND Corporation's report. It was remarkably accurate, but only as far as it went. Winston Baker and his fellow researchers hadn't dug deeply. Conditions were ripe for far more than a mere riot.

Examples of the good life surrounded South Central. To name a few: Malibu, Beverly Hills, Rodeo Drive, Pasadena, the Rose Bowl, Palm Springs, Disneyland, and Hollywood. But surrounded by the American dream, Blacks had been forbidden to participate.

Previous generations had vented their outrage during America's two worst race riots. When their descendants rose

up in fury, Nasheed and his men would turn that protest into a war of independence. He'd be the greatest Black hero ever, and South Central would be free at last.

Nasheed had detected South Central's volatile mood years before Winston Baker had. Unlike RAND researchers, he'd been glad to find the pent-up anger and had done everything he could to encourage it.

When the next riot broke out, Nasheed and his followers would fan the flames. Unaware of him and his intentions, California's government would use minimum force until it was too late.

Victory would be his—along with a prominent place in American history.

CHAPTER SIX
WHITE BLOOD IN THE STREETS

AFTER THE meeting, Larry and his aides sat in overstuffed chairs in his office and opened their briefcases.

"Ted," Larry began, "have you found people with fresh perspectives on South Central?"

"This is my list so far." Roffman tore the top sheet from a notepad and handed it over. "The guy at the top is by far the most interesting."

"Gene Rice," Larry read. "A radio talk show host?"

"A Black talk show host," Roffman corrected, "who argues very effectively that African-Americans won't have equal opportunity without a major change of attitude and behavior."

"What do you think of Mr. Rice, Michael?" Larry asked.

"Whites find his arguments persuasive," Michael replied. "Blacks don't, because he bases his case on the premise that White prejudice has diminished to where it's no longer a significant barrier."

"Is he wrong?" Larry asked.

"That's for you and your Commission to decide."

"You're going sideways on me, Michael. That's not what I need."

"When I was growing up in the South," Michael said, "a White boy ordered me to get off my scooter and let him ride it. When I didn't, he said: 'When a White person tells you to do something, you gotta do it.'

"To him, that was a law of nature. The sun comes up every morning, and Blacks have to do as we're told. These days, not many Whites are that blatant, but Blacks still don't feel equal in a country where flesh-colored crayons aren't the color of *their* skin."

"You're saying that discrimination is still with us, but more subtle?" Larry asked.

"Yes."

"Michael, you're living in the past," Roffman said. "Flesh-colored crayons were renamed. They've been peach for years. Look, Larry, I've got copies of every Gene Rice show since the Tourist Murders began. I'm recording the pertinent segments on a CD so you can listen and make up your own mind about him."

"Finish it this afternoon and I'll listen tonight," Larry said. As Roffman left the room, he told Bridges, "I need a good overview of the Walter Jezierski case—not only what you find on the Internet and in newspapers. Contact reporters and anyone else close to the story."

"I'll get started right away," Michael said. On his way out the door, he handed Larry a book and said, "By the way, that's the book I recommended."

Larry stayed up all night reading the soaring rhetoric and high-minded ideals in *A Nation's Destiny*. When he'd finished, he had a new appreciation of what author Lewis Franklin called America's 'long and terrible history of racism.'

—∞—

The United States had seen some two hundred fifty slave revolts, all abysmal failures. Studying them had provided Muhammad Nasheed with a list of mistakes to avoid.

A South Carolina slave, Jemmy, had taught him not to do what his White enemies anticipated.

In 1739, Jemmy and twenty-some companions marched down a South Carolina road carrying a banner and chanting 'Liberty.' Near the Stono River Bridge, they killed two store employees and armed themselves with muskets and ammunition.

Predictably they next went south toward Spanish-controlled Florida, a haven for fugitive slaves. On the way, they burned plantations, killed two dozen Whites, and were joined by an estimated sixty fellow slaves.

The next day, militiamen caught up with them, sparking a battle in which forty-four slaves were killed. Jemmy and the other survivors continued south. In a second battle—thirty miles away—the slaves were defeated again. Those not killed were captured and executed.

—~—

From the uprising along Louisiana's German Coast, Nasheed learned three lessons: A plan is more important than numbers ... nothing can be accomplished without weapons ... and don't give your enemy time to organize.

In 1811, thirty miles up the Mississippi River from New Orleans, slaves wounded their master and killed his son at the André sugar plantation. Fifteen then marched downriver, past other plantations from which groups joined them.

As they passed larger plantations, their number swelled to an estimated five hundred. By then, they carried flags and marched in cadence to drums. Two days later, they reversed course and headed back upriver.

The largest group of slaves to ever rebel in America wandered aimlessly for two days, allowing volunteer militias, regular troops, and sailors from a U.S. Navy ship to surround them. The slaves fought back with pikes, hoes, axes, and a few firearms.

Before survivors fled into the woods, forty-five slaves were killed. Fifty more were hunted down and decapitated. Their leader, Charles Deslondes, was—in the words of a witness—'put into a bundle of straw and roasted!'

After the rebellion, the severed heads of ninety-five Negroes were put on pikes and displayed along the levee as a warning to other slaves. One observer said they looked, 'like crows sitting on long poles.'

—m—

Denmark Vesey had demonstrated the importance of secrecy.

In 1822, a freedman, Denmark Vesey, was convicted of planning to unleash a secret army of nine thousand slaves, steal arms from military arsenals, then slaughter the White inhabitants of Charleston, South Carolina, and burn the town.

Next they'd commandeer ships and sail to Haiti, the only Black-ruled country in the western hemisphere. This plot was over four years in the making and inspired by Toussaint L'Ouverture's successful Haitian Revolution.

It might have succeeded if slaves, fearing retaliation, hadn't exposed their plan before it could be carried out. Charleston's authorities hanged thirty-five alleged conspirators, including Vesey.

—m—

Studying Nat Turner, Nasheed had seen the danger of staying in one place.

Turner—a Black preacher who believed God had chosen him to free the slaves—and fifty men started a rebellion in 1831, confident that thousands would join them. After killing their master and his family, they seized the Virginia plantation they worked.

For two days, they roamed the surrounding countryside, freeing fellow Blacks and killing sixty White men, women, and children, the largest number of Caucasians to die in a U.S. slave uprising. They used knives, hatchets, axes, and blunt instruments rather than alert other plantations with gunfire.

They should have disappeared into the forests and increased their number by liberating more slaves. A White militia, supported by artillery, crushed the rebellion. Fifty-five of Turner's men were executed, and he got away.

In retaliation, White mobs tortured and murdered two hundred Blacks, more than participated in the rebellion. Militias and sailors from ships anchored in Norfolk killed another hundred Blacks while searching for Turner, who was eventually skinned alive and hanged.

White historians described the killing of three hundred innocent Negroes in dispassionate language, but referred to the murders committed by Turner's men as 'barbarous,' a classic example of victors deciding who'd committed the atrocities.

John Brown had shown that Blacks couldn't rely on help from Whites—not even those who were sympathetic.

In 1859, Brown, a White American abolitionist, led a raid on the federal armory at Harpers Ferry, Virginia, planning to distribute its arms to slaves and lead an insurrection. The attack failed to capture any firearms.

Brown's fleeing men were killed or captured by farmers, militiamen, and U.S. Marines led by Robert E. Lee. Brown was hanged for treason, murder, and inciting an insurrection.

'I learned these lessons well,' Nasheed wrote in his dairy, 'and will soon use them to fill the streets with White blood... or more accurately, red blood from White devils.'

Larry finished Lewis Franklin's book at 10:00 PM that night. Soon afterward, Michael Bridges stuck his head into the room and said, "Looks like you skipped dinner. Shall I order you some?"

"No, thank you. I'm not hungry, having savored every word of this book." Larry held up *A Nation's Destiny*. "What can you tell me about the author?"

"He lives here in Sacramento."

"You're kidding. See if he has time to talk with me tomorrow, will you?"

"Yes, Sir," Michael said. "Anything else?"

"Just one thing. Stop calling me Sir."

"I'll do my best, *Sir.*" Michael smiled and backed out of the room.

He returned a few minutes later to report that Lewis Franklin had agreed to a meeting the next morning.

"Thank you, Michael. Go home and get some rest."

Bridges was halfway out the door when Larry spoke again.

"Reading Franklin's book," he said, "reminded me of the Civil Rights Movement, and the tremendous dignity of the participants. I can still see the composure of Black demonstrators in Selma and Montgomery, the way they dressed, their demeanor. What happened to that?"

"It didn't bring results, and Black people got tired of how one-sided it was."

"A great deal was accomplished," Larry said. "Look at the legislation, the court decisions, and the government programs."

"A lot changed on paper," Michael agreed, "but most Blacks still found it impossible to get fair treatment."

"But things got better, much better. There's been steady progress for at least fifty years."

"To a historian, that sounds good," Michael said, "but to a fifty-year-old Black man, it seems awfully slow, especially since a White man gets those rights and many more, just for being born."

Later, Larry picked up the books Michael brought and stepped into the hallway. Seeing lights in Ted Roffman's office, he looked in. Ted was at his desk with a CD player.

"I've finished editing Gene Rice's recent programs," he said, looking up.

"That was fast," Larry replied. "I'll start listening on my drive home."

"I've read those," Roffman said, pointing at the books cradled in the cook of Larry's arm. "Their authors rehash the long-dead past, complain that Blacks haven't come far since then, and blame Whites. But they fail to mention that Blacks' present-day problems are often self-inflicted."

"See you in the morning," Larry said, turning to go.

Roffman's next words stopped him in his tracks. "Two more tourists were murdered this evening. As usual, the police don't have witnesses or clues."

During his drive home, Larry listened to one of Roffman's CD's. The longer he listened, the more he liked what he heard. But he wasn't ready to suggest inviting Rice to address the Governor's Commission.

The man had no academic credentials, had never held political office, and would have great difficulty persuading the members to take him seriously. His appearance would harden the liberals' attitudes without changing any other minds.

When Larry got home that night, Emily was lying on the couch, looking heartbroken.

"Are you okay?" he asked.

"I'm afraid we've had a miscarriage of sorts," Emily said lifelessly. "The donor mother—God, I hate that name—decided not to give up her baby. New Beginnings says we may have to wait two or more additional years."

Larry had no difficulty sympathizing. Emily had been what she called "nesting" all month. She had bought baby clothes, decorated the nursery, and gone to doctor's appointments with the birth mother. She'd even been present during the ultrasound examination that revealed the baby's gender, female.

"I'll talk with New Beginning's director," Larry said. "I fear I gave him the wrong impression."

He told Emily what the director had said when he'd asked why babies had gone to couples who'd applied after they had.

"I called UC Sacramento," she said, taking his news in stride. "It's too late to cancel my leave of absence and teach this year. I trust your day went better than mine."

"The Race Relations Commission didn't welcome me with open arms," he replied. "Other than that, I had a good day and read a superb book, *A Nation's Destiny* by Lewis Franklin.

Michael arranged for me to talk with him tomorrow morning. I'm looking forward to that."

"Lewis Franklin." Emily faced him. "I'm jealous. I'd give anything to meet him."

"He's coming here. Why don't you sit in on our meeting?"

"I have no business being there," Emily said, "but perhaps you can invite Mr. Franklin to come for dinner sometime."

"Consider it done. By the way, have you ever heard of Walter Jezierski? He's—"

"I know," Emily broke in. "If he's acquitted, it'll probably touch off the riot your Commission hopes to avoid. Does your police background incline you to believe he's innocent?"

"Not at all. It makes me feel he may well be guilty."

Moments after the doorbell rang the next morning, Emily brought a medium-tall, middle-aged, brimming-with-confidence man into Larry's library, and introduced him as Lewis Franklin. He was Black, a possibility that hadn't occurred to Larry as he'd read the man's eloquent prose.

"Surprised I'm Black?" Franklin asked when they were alone. "That happens often since I forbid my publisher to put my picture in my books."

"It's a pleasure to meet you, Mr. Franklin," Larry said, stepping around his desk, hand extended. "I can't tell you how much I enjoyed *A Nation's Destiny*. It's inspiring."

"I should let you change the subject," Franklin said, smiling as they shook hands. "However, you need to understand your reaction was racism, much like that which motivates White men to avoid me by crossing the street and White women to clutch their purses tighter when we're alone in an elevator."

"Make yourself comfortable." Larry gestured to a couch. Rather than sit in the high-backed chair behind his desk, he lowered himself beside Franklin.

"I once asked a White friend if he was more comfortable around mulattoes like me," Franklin said. "He answered that it wasn't my lighter skin and muted features that made him more comfortable with me. It was the beneficial effects of my White genes.

"He meant that exactly as it sounded. He thought Blacks should theoretically have equal opportunity, but feared most didn't work very hard to achieve success. Then he trotted out all those tiresome old statistics about dropping out of school, crime, and illegitimate children."

"Those statistics are tiresome because they've been around too long," Larry said. "By the way, my wife, Emily, is one of your biggest fans. You'll make me a hero in her eyes if you'll come for dinner sometime."

"Is your wife the Emily Winslow who taught at the University of Chicago?"

"One and the same."

"I accept," Franklin said, "on the condition you never tell your friends: 'I have nothing against Black people. I once had Lewis Franklin to dinner in my home.'"

Laughing, Larry asked, "Do you have time this evening?"

"For Emily Winslow, I'll make time."

With attractions like Disneyland, Magic Mountain, and movie studios, Los Angeles had a forty billion dollar a year tourist industry. For decades, this had steadily grown despite the murders of up to fifteen hundred people a year in South Central.

In the past, the dead had been gang members who received scant media attention. But now that some of the victims were White tourists, there was an uproar because fewer tourists were spending money in L.A., adding to the city's economic woes.

Committing multiple murders with police on high alert required almost superhuman patience. Iranian fundamentalists had taught Muhammad Nasheed to back off when things didn't go precisely as planned.

For every tourist murdered, his men gave up on many others because something unexpected happened. So far, there'd been no clues and no witnesses. They had orders to keep it that way.

The basic plan never varied. Nasheed's followers watched car rental desks at L.A. International Airport. When Caucasians identified themselves with passports or out-of-state driver's licenses, their rental vehicle's description was phoned to accomplices at the airport exit.

From there, men in two cars tailed the car. If it didn't get on the freeway that passed through South Central, the cars returned to the airport, and the process began anew with a different intended victim.

As these foreign tourists drove past South Central, one of Nasheed's men in each car folded down the back of its rear seat, worked his upper body into the trunk, and opened a gun port in a tail light. Then one driver pulled in ahead of the rental car and the other got behind it.

Approaching one of the few exits, the man in the lead car's trunk would shoot one of the rental vehicle's tires, using a .17 caliber handgun with a silencer. When the driver pulled over to deal with a seeming blowout, the first car kept going and the second stopped behind the tourists.

"Those are only for short-distance emergency use," the driver—smiling and helpful—would say, pointing at the rental

vehicle's undersized spare tire. "You can get your regular tire repaired at a nearby service station. I'll show you the way. Follow me."

When the tourists agreed, Nasheed's men led them to a stop sign on a quiet street or frontage road. If no one was around, a marksman in the trunk picked off the tourists—including women and children.

—~—

Back when Black crime was the nation's dominant news and politicians ran on law and order platforms, Larry had left the Los Angeles Police Department and gone into business. He had quietly cheered as Blacks began climbing the ladder of success. He'd never doubted they could, but having this proof reassured him.

As a policeman, he'd seen Blacks framed by his fellow officers and convicted by juries easily convinced of their guilt.

The injustice dispensed by America's courts was appalling. Though Blacks were only thirteen percent of the population, they were nearly half the people on death row. Negroes convicted of killing Caucasians were executed at 17 times the rate of Whites convicted of murdering Blacks.

The use of DNA evidence brought about the release of hundreds wrongly convicted of crimes, adding to America's shame.

Studies revealed that half the three thousand people exonerated by this new technology were Black. Innocent Blacks were seven times more likely to be convicted of murder than innocent Whites and only 15% of homicides by Blacks involved White victims.

Later Larry had discovered the deck was stacked against Blacks in other important ways.

A 2009 *Sixty Minutes* episode titled *How accurate is Visual Memory?* began with the 1984 rape of a twenty-two-year-old White college student, Jennifer Thompson. Her assailant, a Black man, had broken into her apartment while she slept and put a knife to her throat.

Determined to identify him for police if she survived, she concentrated on his face and voice, then looked for birthmarks, scars and tattoos.

Circumstantial evidence pointed to Ronald Cotton, and Thompson sealed the case against him by selecting his photo, then picking him out of a lineup. Cotton was sentenced to life plus fifty years.

While in prison, he met Bobby Poole, who'd been convicted of rape and strongly resembled the composite drawing of Jennifer Thompson's assailant. Cotton and Poole worked in the prison kitchen, and the stewards there often mistook one for the other.

A fellow inmate testified he'd heard Poole admit raping Jennifer Thompson. During Cotton's retrial, Thompson—confronted with him and Poole—again chose Cotton as her assailant.

Years later during O.J. Simpson's trial, Cotton heard that DNA was being utilized to release innocent people. A search of the evidence box turned up a fragment of a single sperm. This had viable DNA and proved beyond doubt that Poole was the rapist.

Cotton was released after serving eleven years for a crime he didn't commit. Horrified and guilt-stricken, Thompson arranged to apologize to Cotton at a local church.

"When he walked in," Thompson remembered, "I started to cry and had to sit down or collapse. I told him 'Ron, if I spend every second of the rest of my life telling you how sorry I am, it won't come close to how my heart feels. I'm so sorry.'

"He held my hands and said, 'Jennifer, I don't want you looking over your shoulder. I just want us both to be happy and move on.'"

The two co-authored a book entitled *Picking Cotton*. Together and separately, they campaigned to reform procedures used when obtaining eyewitness testimony. Investigators had told Jennifer that the man she originally identified in the police line-up was the same one whose photograph she'd selected, increasing her confidence that he was the guilty party.

Thanks to Thompson and Cotton, techniques for handling eyewitnesses were improved. New laws mandated that victims be cautioned the perpetrator's photo wasn't necessarily among the photos they were shown. Another required police lineups to be conducted by someone who didn't know who the suspect was.

Thompson and Cotton shared a bond few understood. When they weren't together, they talked frequently by phone. They and their families became friends.

Larry's spirits soared at the end of their *Sixty Minutes* episode. As they hugged at the podium following a joint presentation, he'd felt optimistic about his country's future.

CHAPTER SEVEN
AMERICA'S MOST-ADMIRED MEN

LARRY HAD hired a caterer so Emily could spend the entire evening with Lewis Franklin. Instantly comfortable together, she and he politely included Larry in their conversation until it began moving too quickly.

During a lull, the second course was served and Larry surprised them.

"Would you address the Governor's committee this Thursday?" he asked Franklin.

"Are you sure you want me?" Franklin frowned. "Seems to me our opinions on race relations are quite different. Inviting me to speak must mean you've also invited someone who agrees with you. May I ask who that is?"

"I haven't yet decided," Larry replied.

"I read you're researching another book," Emily broke her silence.

"Yes," Franklin perked up. "I'm thinking of using Black workers who built the Panama Canal as an example of a Black contribution to America's economy made after slaves on its plantations made America an agricultural powerhouse.

"Those men constructed one of the modern world's marvels in one of its most inhospitable jungles and brought the United States huge financial benefits, international prestige, and power.

"Most Americans imagine an army of White men, muscles rippling, braving malaria and yellow fever, succeeding where the French builders of the Suez Canal had failed. The actual labor, however, was done by thirty thousand Blacks, most from the West Indies. They outnumbered their White counterparts fifteen-to-one.

"They get no credit in history books. They were segregated from Whites, given the most dangerous jobs, and were often killed while doing them."

"I've read everything I could find," Larry said, "about Theodore Roosevelt and the building of the Panama Canal. I'd be happy to suggest some books and studies for your research. But I'm afraid they don't substantiate your premise.

"Black canal workers seldom held supervisory positions and never gave orders to Whites. Their housing and facilities were inferior to those for Whites. But you go too far when you say they were abused and cavalierly sent to their deaths."

"It's well documented," Franklin replied, "that four thousand five hundred West Indian workers and only three hundred fifty White Americans died building the canal."

"Most West Indians who died," Larry replied, "were killed by mosquito-borne malaria and yellow fever, or by cholera spread by human feces. Many slept without the provided mosquito netting and removed their window screens to use for other purposes.

"They volunteered to work on the canal where they earned six times what they did at home. They also got plenty to eat, housing superior to any they'd ever had, and free medical care, unheard-of in those days.

"Canal Zone safety standards were higher than those in America. Work was more dangerous for everyone back then.

Thousands of White Americans were killed in mines and factories, and while building dams and bridges.

"Most years, casualties among canal workers were lower than on the workers' home islands. In the final year of construction, thanks to mosquito eradication and quinine, the death rate was below that of the healthiest U.S. state."

"You may have just spoiled a promising idea," Franklin said good-naturedly. "May I please have a list of your sources?"

"I fear Ted Roffman is right," Emily said when she and Larry were in bed that night. "You've invited the wrong man to address the Race Relations Commission."

"Why do you say that?" he asked.

"Franklin's attention is riveted on the past. For two hours we discussed the program I'm preparing for possible use in South Central, but all he wanted to talk about was the history of the problem."

"At worst," Larry said, "he'll give us a history lesson, which isn't nearly as bad as what will happen if I un-invite him."

"Do you think Governor Webster really wants me to advise the Commission?"

"It doesn't matter," Larry replied. "I'm in charge, and I want you."

"I worry that involving me is another of your attempts to improve our relationship."

"I freely admit it."

Looking sad, she said, "Nothing has changed since the last time we failed."

Back then they'd agreed their problem wasn't the presence of bad times but the absence of good ones.

—∿—

When Larry arrived Friday morning, the Governor's conference room smelled of furniture polish and Ted Roffman was talking with several Commission members. He took Larry aside.

"Why'd you invite Lewis Franklin as the first speaker?" he asked quietly. "The Commission's recommendations will be the same old same old if you don't give them both sides of the story. You should've started with Gene Rice."

"Find me a scholar," Larry said, "not a talk show host."

"There are several on the list I gave you, but none is as persuasive as Rice."

"What makes you like him so much?"

"Being Black, he gets away with pointing out facts no White non-racist would touch with a ten-foot pole."

Sacramento was having a rare summer storm, but the rain had stopped and the thunder was now a distant rumble. Larry called the meeting to order and introduced Lewis Franklin.

Franklin approached the lectern and set his briefcase on it. The Commission's twelve members—except Avery King—turned on laptop computers or smartphones. Larry called the meeting to order, introduced Lewis Franklin, and clapped until everyone joined in.

"This Commission's purpose is to promote racial understanding," Franklin began, "yet you have voluntarily segregated yourselves, Blacks and two Hispanics on one side, Whites and two Hispanics on the other. To reach all of you, I'd have to deliver three different speeches."

Looking to his right, he said, "If I were speaking to only the people who look like me, I'd talk about the partnership between Blacks and Whites and how it brought America closer to racial equality.

"I'd remind you that the Civil Rights Movement was necessary because of White racists, but wouldn't have achieved its successes without support from thousands of other Whites. I'd tell you we shouldn't allow that partnership to fall apart. If we're left to sink or swim on our own, we'll sink."

Franklin shifted his gaze to the table's other side. "But if I gave that speech here, you Whites would congratulate yourselves on a job well done. 'What do they want now?' you'd wonder. The answer is: 'We no longer want to be *they*.'"

Franklin took photographs from his briefcase.

"These," he continued, "were taken in 1957 by a *Life* magazine photographer in Little Rock, Arkansas. They show an angry White mob attempting to prevent nine African-American children from integrating Central High School after the Supreme Court's Brown vs. Board of Education decision.

"That mob was restrained from attacking those children by the Alabama National Guard, which kept peace at Central High for a year. One of the Black students, Thelma Mothershed, said there were days when so many Whites spit on her that she could wring spittle from her skirt."

Dolores Menke, a White business owner from Los Angeles, raised her hand. Franklin nodded in response.

"That mob didn't get its way," she said, "because the majority of Whites wanted to do the right thing."

"The majority?" Franklin cupped his hand to his ear like an eavesdropper in a farce. "I beg to disagree. Orval Faubus, the governor of Arkansas, closed Little Rock's schools for a year to stop further integration. Racism was his only claim to fame, and his message resonated from coast to coast.

"A 1958 Gallup Poll named him as one of the ten most admired men in America—along with Sir Winston Churchill,

Dr. Albert Schweitzer, General Douglas MacArthur, Dr. Jonas Salk, and President Dwight Eisenhower."

"There are racists in the Black community, as well," Menke said.

"Can you give me an example of how Black racism has hurt you?"

"Yes, but I'd rather tell you how it's hurt Blacks. When in high school, I worked in the Head Start program, tutoring Black preschoolers. Their test scores improved dramatically until their parents demanded that Head Start send *ethnic* instructors."

Franklin took more pictures from his briefcase.

"These," he said, "show White mobs and policemen beating peaceful Black demonstrators during the Civil Rights Movement. The police used cattle prods, tear gas, bullwhips, dogs, and fire hoses so powerful they could knock people down and skid them along the street.

"White mobs used chains, baseball bats, ax handles, pipes, rubber tubing wrapped with barbed wire, even guns. Hundreds of those they beat had fought in World War II and Korea, yet couldn't avail themselves of America's most basic rights."

"I believe my hiring practices," Menke said, "better reflect today's attitudes. I voluntarily hire a higher percentage of Blacks than the government requires."

"Believe me, I know there are people like you," Franklin said. "They, however, are busy with their own families and lives. If America is to ever live up to its ideals, we need more of their help."

Franklin reached into his briefcase and brought forth a sheaf of photocopies.

"In the mid-1970s," he said, "Hank Aaron was zeroing in on baseball's most hallowed record, Babe Ruth's 714 lifetime home runs. As he got closer, his hate mail skyrocketed. There were so many death threats that the *Atlanta Journal* secretly wrote his obituary."

Ron Jardine, the Commission's other Caucasian stood and said, "There's more to that story. At that time, Aaron was receiving 3,000 letters a week, most from well-wishers and admirers. Babe Ruth's widow publicly denounced the hate mail and told the world her husband would've cheered Aaron on."

"Do you think that made him feel any better?" Franklin asked.

"No. But these days, White sports fans idolize Black athletes. My son plays basketball and dreams of playing like Michael Jordan—not Larry Bird."

Taking control of the discussion, Franklin continued, "The National Association for the Advancement of Colored People did a study and determined that approximately five thousand Blacks were lynched between Reconstruction and the modern civil rights movement."

Typing on her smartphone with one hand, Dolores Menke raised her hand. Franklin pointed at her with his chin.

"Tuskegee Institute, a respected Black university," she read from her screen, "has kept lynching statistics since the late 1800s. They determined the total number was 4,743."

"An estimate," Franklin countered, "which I couldn't remember and rounded off at 5,000."

"Yes," Menke replied, "but a quarter of those lynched were White, and I haven't heard of even one lynching in my lifetime. These days, ninety percent of South Central's murder victims are killed by other Blacks."

"There have been both legal and illegal lynchings in our lifetimes," Franklin corrected. "In 1944, 14-year-old George Stinney Jr. was electrocuted for killing two White girls, becoming the youngest American executed in the 20th century. During his two-hour trial there was little or no cross-examination of prosecution witnesses or calling of defense witnesses. The all-White, all-male jury took just 10 minutes to find Stinney guilty. When sentenced to death, he was barely over 5 feet and weighed 95 pounds. He fit in the electric chair by sitting on a Bible.

"In 2014, a circuit court judge threw out Stinney's conviction.

"In 1955, fourteen-year-old Emmett Till was tortured and lynched after a White woman accused him of grabbing her and making crude sexual remarks. After Till was lynched and tortured, he was shot in the head and his corpse was thrown into the Tallahatchie River.

"He'd been so horribly mutilated that his mother insisted on an open casket funeral so the American public would be aware of the terrible suffering inflicted on her son by a lynch mob.

"Emmett's murderers were never brought to justice, and years later, his accuser admitted she'd lied.

"With the advent of cell phones, these so-called honor crimes were weaponized into a sinister new form by White women who called 911 to report Black men for harassing them, when in fact those men had been bird watching, walking, or something equally innocuous.

"Black lynchings were notably barbaric and happened throughout the country—not only in southern and border states. Police officers often participated. There was absolutely no evidence against at least a third of the victims, and none had the benefit of a trial."

Aloud, Franklin read an account of a 1930s lynching, written by a White newsman: "'After being unsexed, the victim was forced to eat that portion of his anatomy, then was chained to a lever and sadistically lowered into and raised from a bonfire until burned to a crisp.'"

Franklin took more photos from his briefcase.

"These," he said, "are copies of a few of the pictures displayed at the New York Historical Society in 2000. They show Blacks, sometimes in groups, being hanged, burned alive, or dismembered. Sponsors of these spectacles put up posters advertising them, charged admission and, for a fee, allowed spectators to pose for pictures with the corpses.

"Like Mrs. Menke and Mr. Jardine, many White Americans honestly believe racism is no longer a serious problem in this country. When you see these pictures, do you believe these people's children and grandchildren regard Blacks as equals?

"Or are they employers who tell Blacks no jobs are available and hire a White person ten minutes later? Or landlords who tell Black families they rented their last apartment, then offer a White family its choice of six?"

When finished, Franklin received a standing ovation. Clearly Dolores Menke and Ron Jardine were applauding the man—not his message.

CHAPTER EIGHT
DIFFERENT VERSIONS OF THE TRUTH

WHILE LEWIS Franklin's visual aids circulated, Larry called a recess and sat down beside Horace Grayson, the Commission's Black Ph.D. He caught a glimpse of a lynching photo and wished he hadn't. Closing his eyes didn't erase the memory of the dangling, charred corpse of a Black man hanged with a chain, doused with gasoline, and set on fire.

"I'm ready to discuss the Walter Jezierski case," Larry said quietly.

"I didn't expect that subject to resurface," Grayson responded, "until I raised it myself."

"It's difficult for me to make the transition from that photograph to polite conversation."

"When you've seen as many as I have," Grayson said, "they enrage rather than horrify you."

"Hope I never see another."

"If you were Black, you'd want everyone to see them. Perhaps after seeing victims of our holocaust, Whites will understand what Martin Luther King meant when he said ending racial hatred will free the Black man's body and the White man's soul." Grayson rubbed his eyes. "What have you learned about Walter Jezierski so far?"

"He's a White police officer," Larry began, "with several commendations for bravery and numerous complaints alleging excessive force against Blacks. Last year, he shot Marcus Brown, a Black teenager, to death while apprehending him after a drive-by shooting.

"Witnesses say Jezierski didn't have to shoot Brown. His partner swears he had no choice. Jezierski's lawyer wants to move the trial to Orange County. If he succeeds, Black activists fear an all-White jury will acquit, setting off the riot we're trying to prevent. That's it in a nutshell."

"This case is too big for a nutshell," Grayson said gently. "The devil's in the details even more than usual."

—𝔪—

"What do you think will happen when the Jezierski case goes to trial?" Larry asked Grayson as their discussion continued during lunch.

"Odds are," Grayson replied, "that an all-White jury would acquit, believing Jezierski thought Brown had a gun. An all-Black jury would almost certainly convict, theorizing that Jezierski decided to execute Brown rather than bring him in for trial. And a mixed jury will be unable to render a verdict."

"The brutality of the Los Angeles Police Department," Grayson changed subjects, "and your having been an LAPD officer were my reasons for opposing your appointment to head this Commission."

He held up both hands, stopping Larry from interrupting.

"That, I'm sorry to say, was a classic example of prejudice leading to the wrong conclusions. I strongly suspect that, when you were a policeman, you saw things that won't let you believe Jezierski's necessarily innocent."

Larry called the meeting back to order. The subsequent discussion of Walter Jezierski's upcoming trial produced the already familiar seven-to-three split, with Dolores Menke, Ron Jardine, and Larry being the three.

"You shouldn't have led off with Lewis Franklin," Ted groused when he, Emily, Larry, and Bridges were back in Larry's office. "We have to hear from all sides, of course, but the first speaker sets the tone. If you want your version of the truth to prevail you have to get in the game—not stand on the sideline."

"Have you finished recording the highlights from Gene Rice's radio shows?"

"Yes," Roffman replied, "and you needn't worry. I gave you examples of his controversial statements as well as the ones with which any reasonable person would agree."

Emily and Larry sat closer than usual in the limousine's rear seat as Don Maxwell drove them home after the meeting.

"Ted Roffman recorded highlights from Gene Rice's radio show," Larry said, taking CDs from his briefcase. "During the programs I've heard so far, I thought Rice acquitted himself well."

"That's not surprising," Emily said, "considering that Ted Roffman chose them."

That evening and early the following morning, Larry listened to more of Gene Rice's broadcasts.

"White attitudes are unchanged," the first caller declared, "since the days when Black demonstrators were beaten during the Civil Rights Movement."

"Let's examine your statement," Rice responded. "Back then, hundreds of policemen brutally beat thousands of peaceful demonstrators and went unpunished. More recently the beating of one Black man, Rodney King—who had, in fact, broken the law—brought a national outcry from millions of Whites and—"

"Yeah," the caller interrupted, "but a White jury found the policemen innocent."

"After which," Rice countered, "the federal government filed charges. In that second trial, two of the four officers were convicted."

"Say what you will," the next caller began, "we Blacks have difficulty getting decent jobs because we're considered lazy."

"I hate it," Rice responded, "when people assume I'm lazy because of my color. So I prove them wrong with my hard work. Too many African-Americans are so resentful that they do the opposite.

"A report on KTLA last night featured the Black owner of a landscaping company. He started out hiring Blacks exclusively. Now he hires only Mexicans, claiming they work harder."

"How can you doubt it's more difficult for Blacks to succeed?" another caller asked. "Marian Anderson, a singer, is an example. While in high school, she applied to a music school and was rejected with a curt: 'We don't take Colored.'

"Later she was barred from singing at the better U.S. venues. Nonetheless, she became known as the world's greatest contralto singer. By 1939, she'd performed for millions throughout the world, representing her country and her race with dignity and grace."

"When she was denied the right to sing at Constitution Hall in Washington, D.C.," Rice countered, "First Lady

Eleanor Roosevelt resigned from the Daughters of the American Revolution, which owned the hall. Then with the help of Secretary of the Interior Harold Ickes, she arranged a concert at the Lincoln Memorial.

"On an Easter Sunday, it was attended by a live audience of seventy-five thousand people, twenty times more than would have heard her in Constitution Hall. She opened with *America*. You know, 'My country 'tis of thee, sweet land of liberty, of thee I sing…'

"During her illustrious career, Anderson sang in Carnegie Hall, Constitution Hall, at the Hollywood Bowl, and on the Ed Sullivan Show. Named radio's foremost woman singer for six consecutive years, she also sang the national anthem at the inaugurations of Dwight Eisenhower and John F. Kennedy.

"If she did all that back when Negroes had to step off the sidewalk for Whites, what can we accomplish now—after affirmative action, school bussing, and the like?

"According to *Forbes* Magazine, there are fifteen Black Americans worth between $125 million and $2.7 billion dollars. America also has 109,000 Black households with a net worth of over a million dollars."

Larry liked what he'd heard and listened to more the following morning. Before breakfast he dialed his cell phone.

"You win," he said when Ted Roffman answered. "Call Gene Rice and ask if he'll come to Sacramento for an off-the-record interview."

—∞—

The murder of three more tourists was the lead news story that evening. A Black police officer had come upon the crime while it was in progress. His efforts had saved two of the intended victims, but he'd been shot dead. Within hours, police had arrested gang members dubbed "the Los Angeles Seven."

By midnight, the case against them had fallen apart. Released, the Seven walked into pandemonium outside the police station. Despite the late hour, they didn't seem surprised by the number of journalists, television cameras, and klieg lights.

"Don't be surprised if a riot in South Central spreads to White neighborhoods," their spokesman told reporters.

KTLA's news director, Brian Waterman, whispered to his cameraman, "Someone helped that guy memorize his little speech. This whole spectacle was orchestrated. One minute the police had an airtight case against those guys. Two hours later they turn them loose.

"It's like someone planted evidence they knew wouldn't stand up to scrutiny. Something similar happened before the Watts Riot. Tensions were high and pillars of the Black community asked for calm at a public meeting.

"Then a young Black agitator stepped up to the microphone and predicted a riot would bring death and destruction to Black and White communities alike. He was escorted from the hall, and subsequent speakers disavowed what he'd said. Guess which speech was on television that night.

"The next day, Whites lined up outside gun stores that sold out in less than three hours. That was spontaneous, but this was orchestrated. By whom and why?"

—∾—

The Los Angeles Seven had been worth every penny Muhammad Nasheed paid them. Bigots of every stripe were calling talk shows to express their unvarnished opinions of other races. Caucasians were armed to the teeth. South Central was exactly where Nasheed wanted it ... on edge.

He sat at his computer, adding to the file where he'd recorded his plans and deeds for five years. To make his diary inconspicuous, he'd typed it on ledger pages in an accounting program, fitting since it was a record of a long overdue account he intended to collect.

Keeping a diary violated everything Nasheed had been taught in Iran. But he added to it only when alone, and it was protected by an explosive device which would destroy his computer and kill anyone who turned it on without disarming it.

Soon the world would know him by his Muslim name, Muhammad Nasheed. After that he'd never again use his hated Christian name, Jamal King.

CHAPTER NINE
GENE RICE

TO FURTHER explore the possibility of having Gene Rice address the Governor's Commission, Larry called the radio talk show star at his Los Angeles home.

"Would you be interested," he began, "in coming to Sacramento incognito and addressing the Governor's Commission on Race Relations? You can stay at my house. I'd like your appearance to be unannounced in advance. If Avery King catches wind of it, he'll ignite a firestorm of protest. I'd prefer to avoid that and… "

"Say no more," Rice replied. "I'll do it. It's unlikely anyone will recognize me. My audience knows my voice but not what I look like. Besides, all us Black people look alike." He chuckled.

Gene Rice reminded Larry of Bill Cosby before the latter's sexual scandals and fall from grace. His voice and grammar didn't reveal his race. Nor did the contents of his mind. Wondering what had shaped this unique man, Larry theorized that Whites had raised Rice. It turned out he'd been brought up by his natural parents, still married and Black.

At dinner, Larry sat quietly while Emily and Rice discussed race, each expressing opinions normally held by people of the other's race.

At 4:00 AM Larry woke and began reading in his study. Half an hour later Rice was awake and noticed the light.

"Looks like we're both insomniacs," he said, announcing his presence from the doorway.

Larry closed his book, placed both hands on the desk and interlocked his fingers.

"Hope I didn't wake you," he said. "Five hours sleep is all I need. I've never met another Black man like you,"

"If my assumption is correct," Rice continued, "you haven't met many Blacks except during your years with LAPD. In that line of work, you wouldn't have met many like me. I'm law abiding."

Emily cleared her throat to advise them they weren't alone.

After breakfast Don Maxwell drove the three of them to the State Capitol Building. Once in the governor's conference room, Rice sat down and read articles written by that afternoon's guest on his show. After the Commission's members arrived he placed a printed sheet in front of each one.

No one recognized Rice but all knew who he was after Larry introduced him.

"America has evolved," Rice began with his no-nonsense style and without notes. "Black people can now do well here. Wherever you look there are successful Black doctors, lawyers, business owners, movie directors, clergymen, professors, and one who authored a book on Greek syntax and grammar.

"A NASA space shuttle was commanded by a Black astronaut, and we've had a Black president.

"Ominously, however, nearly seventy-five percent of all Black babies are illegitimate. Only twelve percent of Black households are headed by both parents, because the men didn't accept responsibility for these children, leaving the women to take care of that.

"Someone—a Black man I'd guess—famously boasted, 'Once you go Black, you'll never go back,' referring to a woman's choice of sexual partners. He could have more accurately said, 'Once you go Black, you're a single mom.'

"Blacks have America's lowest grades and highest dropout rate. More Black males under thirty are incarcerated than in college. In that same age group, murder is the number one cause of death. Ninety-four percent of those murders are committed by other Blacks.

"In light of these statistics, it's crazy to blame racism for all of South Central's problems, and—"

"You spout statistics but don't give us sources," King interrupted.

"The source of every statistic I just quoted is on the list I passed out," Rice continued. "People succeed when they act in their best interests. Unfortunately, in Los Angeles too many Blacks are conditioned to fail by friends, parents, and even their leaders.

"They're told they'll fail no matter how hard they try. They tell each other school is a waste of time because Whites won't permit them to use their educations.

"Children in Black ghettos are taught hopelessness the way other kids are taught positive thinking. They become adults who protest the way they're portrayed on television and in movies, ignoring research that proves they're portrayed as successful at a higher rate and as criminals at a lower rate than they actually are."

"Why slander your own people," King blurted out when Rice paused.

"Oprah Winfrey said much the same after being criticized for building her Leadership Academy for disadvantaged girls in South Africa rather than here. She said she'd asked girls in our inner-city what they wanted, and they'd asked for iPads and expensive sneakers.

Then Rice read from a newspaper clipping: "Oprah said: 'In South Africa, they ask for uniforms so they can go to school—'"

"I was among those," King cut him off again, "who thought she'd become a billionaire in America and should've put her school here."

"Apparently she wanted to invest her money in people eager to help themselves and—."

"If racism is dead in America," King interrupted again, "how do you—?"

"I don't deny America's continuing racism," Rice said, reclaiming control. "However, at a time when Black politicians are being elected in overwhelmingly White districts, prejudice has declined to where we can overcome it by calling attention to subtle racism as well as the blatant kind. Let me give you some examples.

"All My Baby Mamas" was a proposed reality T.V program featuring Black rapper Shawty Lo along with ten Black women and eleven children he fathered with them. Responding to the outrage provoked by the first episode, the Parents Television Council condemned the show as 'irresponsible, exploitative, and perverse' and forced its cancellation.

"Other degrading of Black women included a repulsive blog on which men discussed techniques for exposing their genitals to women. In mid-2011, this website urged its followers to target Black women, falsely claiming they were oversexed and might not report such activities."

"During slavery," Rice continued, "it was a right of passage for White Plantation owners to require mature Black female slaves to have sex with their teenage White sons. The theory was that Black women were good teachers who'd prepare those White sons to sexually satisfy their future White wives.

"After slavery was outlawed, this practice continued in former slave states, sending demeaning messages to Black girls."

"I wish I'd invited the media to hear Mr. Rice," Larry whispered to Ted Roffman. "He's saying things that should be heard beyond this room."

"Mr. Rice," Avery King continued, "think of the good a man with an audience the size of yours could do by giving the Black community a positive message."

"What more positive message could I give?" Rice asked. "Every day, I tell young Blacks they can succeed if they stay in school, study, get good grades, stay away from alcohol and drugs, and wait to start their families until they're married and financially ready.

"Would you prefer I tell them there's no hope, no opportunity, and no point in trying? Even if I'm wrong, who's giving a more positive message? I tell the next generation of Black youths they'll be rewarded if they prepare themselves. You tell them any effort they make will be nullified.

"The despair that comes from believing they have no future is the reason suicide is the third highest cause of death among young Black males."

"Mr. Rice," Dr. Grayson said gently. "There's a great deal of truth in what you say, but it would've improved your presentation if—instead of referring to *Blacks*—you'd said *some Blacks*."

"I stand corrected." Rice smiled. "Thank you. You're absolutely right and I freely admit it."

CHAPTER TEN
TESTING THE WATER WITH BOTH FEET

Blacks hadn't earned America's respect. They'd been too docile for too long. No other group on earth had ever been suppressed so effortlessly. For three centuries, they'd built America's economy without credit, respect, or pay.

After their emancipation, they'd continued to do America's dirty work as sharecroppers for next to nothing. And throughout this centuries-long nightmare, first brutal slave owners and then the Ku Klux Klan had made them afraid to follow the example of Toussaint L'Ouverture and other courageous Haitians.

Later America's Blacks had been kept in line with a thimbleful of welfare here, a teaspoon of rights there, the title of 'a credit to your race,' and Christian advice to turn the other cheek.

Outnumbered ten-to-one, Blacks would never win an all-out war against their oppressors. But they could do what a Masai tribe in Africa did in the mid-nineteenth century. After the first skirmish with British Imperial troops, the Masai chief refused to sign the proposed treaty.

Then his warriors attacked the invaders. They didn't attempt to hold ground or achieve the usual military objectives. They simply killed as many of their enemies as possible. When the outnumbered British began withdrawing, the Masai chief went to their camp and signed the treaty he'd rejected.

"Why did you order your men to fight," the British general had asked, "only to sign the treaty when you were winning?"

"I know how the British fight," the remarkably frank old chief replied. "You continue to send more fighters until you win. I didn't want you to see us as a conquered people. I wanted you to dread fighting us again."

Instead of showing such courage, most of America's Blacks waited for Abraham Lincoln to free them. And now thousands of them were trapped in South Central, watching immigrants pass through on the way to better lives.

Shopkeepers in South Central's Koreatown were the first newcomers to establish businesses there. Since then, they'd acquired a reputation for preying on Black customers and were hated because several had shot Black youths they'd said were stealing.

During the Watts and Rodney King Riots, Korean shopkeepers had held looters at bay with assault rifles. But when the next riot broke out, the looters would also have military weapons, and they'd gain respect like the Masai before them, with the lives of their warriors.

—∞—

During its eleventh meeting, Governor Webster's Commission deviated from its planned itinerary. Instead it discussed the previous night's so-called Koreatown *disturbance,* which had claimed eight lives.

A Korean merchant had shot and killed two Black teenagers who'd broken into his electronics store after midnight. He told police he'd thought these intruders had guns and in defense of his family—asleep above the store—he'd shot them.

Twenty LAPD officers had been needed to escort the Korean and his family through an angry mob pelting them with bottles, insults, and threats. Later, cars were overturned and torched. By the time fire engines arrived, Wilshire Boulevard was an obstacle course.

As firefighters extinguished vehicle fires and pushed still-smoking hulks aside with their trucks, a sniper wounded two. Their companions retreated to safety and watched flames spread from Korean businesses to others that were Black-owned.

"We came to save their businesses, and they shot at us," a fireman complained to reporters, assuming the snipers owned the burning stores.

Later, armed gang members assaulted a number of Korean-owned businesses. During the Rodney King riot, those owners had successfully defended their stores. This time, the attackers set them afire.

When calm had been restored, an LAPD captain told reporters, "To my knowledge, the Crips and Bloods have never participated in social unrest. All they care about is their multi-million dollar drug trade. This attack was led by someone familiar with sophisticated military tactics and weapons."

Larry was ushered into the office of Lieutenant General Edward Nelson, commander of California's National Guard. During their earlier phone conversation Nelson had offered to meet at Larry's office.

"I'm sure you have more than enough on your plate after being put on alert," Larry had responded, "I'll go to you."

General Nelson was tall, square-jawed, and gray-haired. He'd been a colonel when the Guard responded to the Rodney King Riot in 1992.

"I was inspired by your book about the military's elimination of the color barrier," Larry said as they shook hands. "You must be proud of your role."

"Very," Nelson replied. "When our armed forces went from racially troubled to color-blind it was America's most successful desegregation."

"I came," Larry said, "to ask if you'll address Governor Webster's Commission on preventing another riot in South Central."

Nelson gestured for Larry to sit with him on a sofa.

"We succeeded," he continued, "because we didn't pretend to make Blacks equal. We actually did it. Unfortunately, there are no parallels between what we did and what you hope to do. The military's not a microcosm of society. We can refuse undesirables or discharge them, giving us control politicians don't have."

"I've read," Larry continued, "that when the Guard was in South Central for the Rodney King Riot, there was no crime and hundreds of residents begged them to stay longer."

"Yes," Nelson said warily.

"I'm thinking of asking the Commission to recommend that if Governor Webster sends your men in, he should leave them a while."

"Save your breath," Nelson said. "That would be political suicide, which is what it'll be for you if your Commission recommends it. Remember when Jimmy the Greek lost his job as a sportscaster?"

"Vividly."

"All he did was speculate that Blacks are superior athletes because slave owners bred them for physical strength and endurance. Auctioneers selling them routinely pointed out their physical attributes, and stressed their bloodlines the way they do with horses nowadays."

Abruptly he handed Larry a printed sheet.

"That," he explained, "is a copy of a letter I sent Governor Webster some time ago. In the event of a riot, I'm hoping he'll forbid live broadcasts from that area. When people see or hear of looting, they run to where the action is.

"Also I want to deploy a large number of armored personnel carriers this time. The Guard sets up barricades to inhibit people's movement during riots. Those are where the civilian deaths usually occur because people don't follow instructions or appear to have aggressive intentions. When soldiers are in or behind APC's, they're better able to hold their fire.

"One more thing. My aide, Tony Jackson, is a Black ex-gang member with a degree in sociology. He has an impressive record of getting kids out of gangs and plenty of ideas for improving the situation in South Central. I'll assign him to you for a few days if you want."

CHAPTER ELEVEN
BUILDING A DAM DURING A FLOOD

TONY JACKSON had perfect posture, movie star looks, and was all soldier. He couldn't suppress a smile when Don Maxwell drove up in the Lieutenant Governor's high performance Lincoln MKZ sedan.

"Want to drive it?" Larry asked.

"You're kidding!" Jackson exclaimed.

"Give him the keys, Don," Larry told his bodyguard.

"May I see your driver's license and insurance card?' Maxwell asked, adding, "Take them out of your wallet, please."

Sitting beside Jackson, Larry was silent until they'd merged into freeway traffic.

"General Nelson," he began, "tells me you have no end of ideas for improving conditions in South Central."

"May I speak freely, Sir?" Jackson asked.

"Please do," Larry replied. "Now and always."

"General Nelson ordered me to take this assignment," Jackson said. "I don't want it."

"Why not? It could be an opportunity to put some of your ideas into practice."

"If that happened, by some miracle," Jackson scoffed, "my ideas would be watered down and unrecognizable."

"Give me an example," Larry encouraged.

"Okay." Jackson grinned. "If I had my way, I'd bring back the draft. Universal Military Service used to give young Black men two things many of them need—skills and discipline."

Chuckling, Larry asked, "How'd you go from being a gang member to advocating *that*?"

"I wasn't accepted anywhere because I had a White mother and a Black father," Jackson began. "After mom skipped out, my father worked two jobs and I was alone most days.

"I was twelve when the Crips offered me a place to belong and cool friends who protected me and kept me safe. I couldn't have been more comfortable until the day I was handed a gun and taken into the Bloods' territory to avenge the murder of a fellow Crip. I couldn't bring myself to pull the trigger.

"A Black minister named Culpepper got me out of the gangs by teaching me productive hatred. He said racists point to the behavior of some Blacks to prove we're all inferior. When one Black ditches school, they call us all uneducated baboons. If one of us sticks a knife in someone, they call us all savages.

"Culpepper encouraged me to prove racists wrong by making something of myself. Doors open for you when there's something in your wallet besides fake ID. But to achieve success, Blacks need the extra energy provided by productive hatred. For most Black gang members, the hatred is already there, but instead of using it productively they become what racists say they are."

"How'd you wind up in the Guard?"

"After leaving the gangs," Jackson answered, "I needed another place to belong. First, I joined the Nation of Islam, the Black Muslims. I liked their emphasis on discipline and Black pride, but they also advocate violence. Since there aren't many jobs for Black sociology majors, the military was a logical next step."

They stopped at a coffee shop for lunch.

"When were you a policeman?" Tony asked Larry.

"Thirty years ago," Larry replied.

"South Central has changed since then. Life is better for most. But there are thousands of young gang members with subhuman morals. They're another breed that exists on the fringes of the human experience. By the time they're in their teens, most are beyond help or dead."

Tony turned into a bad neighborhood, and proceeded after Larry overruled Don Maxwell's objection. Farther along, he parked near four young Black men in football jerseys, faces oozing hostility. Their expressions didn't soften until Tony got out of the car and was recognized.

"Wassup, Niggah?" one asked.

His voice completely different, Tony said something Larry didn't understand.

Larry had confronted gang members before, but these were—as Tony had said—another breed by several orders of magnitude.

Tony pointed with his chin at the man who'd just spoken.

"This is Kareem," he told Larry in his normal voice. "He says he might meet with the Governor he saw on television, but not you."

After another exchange with Kareem, Tony translated again.

"He wants you to put it in your report that America will be better after Whites go back to Europe. He also said that when the next riot breaks out, he and his friends will go to Los Angeles and participate."

—~—

"Does that boy honestly believe the things he said?" Don Maxwell asked as he drove the Lincoln back toward a world he understood.

"That was the tip of the iceberg," Tony replied. "Some of his beliefs make a certain kind of sense. He thinks U.S. Courts have no jurisdiction over him because his ancestors were brought here against their will... and that he's not subject to military service because that's a duty of citizenship, the benefits of which he's been denied.

"But he and thousands like him believe AIDS was developed in a laboratory by Whites and intentionally introduced into their community. They're also convinced birth control is a scheme to keep Blacks in the minority, where they can be outvoted... and that education is a plot to make them docile and easy to suppress.

"I once thought like those boys do. I felt powerful when the Crips gave me a gun and told me to fire a shot into the ground. Instantly people cleared the street. Windows slammed shut and doors were locked.

"Soon I was on a slippery downhill slope, selling drugs. I made far more money than my father did working two jobs. I lived in the present and gave no thought to the future. I figured I'd be dead before I was twenty.

"The boys we just left are the fourth generation to grow up during the war between the Crips and Bloods. Some haven't been more than a mile from home. I'd love to set up programs that take them places where young people are preparing for interesting professions, looking forward to long lives, and having fun.

"The other day I read a study that compared twelve-year-old twin Black brothers, adopted and raised in different families.

"The one brought up in an integrated neighborhood had a good self-image and a college scholarship. His twin—raised in South Central—was self-destructive, anti-social, violent, and spoke a language unintelligible outside the ghetto. He'd already been in trouble with the law and had dropped out of school.

"If there's a riot and the Guard goes into South Central, we should stay there long enough to break the cycle of violence."

"General Nelson and I," Larry said, "were discussing that subject when he suggested I talk to you. Actually, I was trying to discuss it. He wouldn't."

"Doing that," Tony said, "could get him relieved of his command."

"What would you have the Guard do," Larry pressed, "if there's another riot and they stay afterward?"

"Create a safe environment. Those kids are surrounded by violence and bad role models. The Guard could keep schools open late so students would be in a safe environment until there's an adult at home.

"We could run sports programs after school and on weekends. We could offer tutoring, have tradesmen teach their skills. The list is endless. Problem is ... no governor will ever have the political courage to use the Guard that way."

CHAPTER TWELVE
SOCIALIZED TO BE SELF-DESTRUCTIVE

WHEN LARRY returned to his office, Ted Roffman and Michael Bridges were hard at work.

"Brian Waterman sent some footage KTLA shot last night in Koreatown," Ted began. "He thought your Commission should see what it's dealing with."

Michael slid a disc into a DVD player, and images of buildings—flames leaping from their windows—appeared on screen. He fast forwarded to a rampaging mob setting fire to parked cars. Nearby, looters were streaming through the smashed doors of an electronics store.

Two policemen drove up as a teenage girl came out, pushing an overloaded shopping cart.

"Leave that cart where it is and go home immediately," an officer bellowed through a bullhorn.

Glaring at him, the girl sped up screaming, "You don't scare me, motherfucker. They won't let you shoot us. We're not armed."

Grabbing a box, she turned and sprinted into the spectators.

The next scene showed the Korean merchant who'd shot Black intruders in his shop. Policemen had taken him and his family into protective custody and were escorting them through a barrage of profanity and bottles.

Near their cars a woman blocked their path. Her face twisted with hate, spittle flying from her mouth, she screamed, "Let us kill this worthless piece of shit. He murdered my son. I wanna see his fucking brains all over the sidewalk."

"Turn it off," Larry said wearily. "I've had enough gritty truth for one day. Ask Brian Waterman if he'll make us a compilation of KTLA's interviews with South Central residents who didn't want the Guard to leave after the Rodney King Riot. I'd like to talk with them."

—w—

As always, Larry slept five hours that night. At 3:00 he tiptoed to his library, leaving Emily asleep in their bed. Three hours later, he finished studying Tony Jackson's recommendations on how the Guard might be used if it went into South Central.

On his way to shower and dress for breakfast, he passed Emily in the hallway.

"Good morning," she greeted him, her voice serious. "If you have a free moment before leaving for work, I'd like to talk about something."

"I too have something I'd like to discuss," Larry replied cheerfully. "There's no time like the present. Lead the way."

He followed Emily to their bed where he sat while she lay on her side, supporting her upper body on one elbow.

"You first," he said.

"No, you. Please."

"Back in the early 1900s," Larry began, "George Ferguson documented that Blacks consistently score fifteen percent below Whites on standard intelligence tests. In the century since then, that difference has persisted despite the use of tests written especially for Blacks."

"IQ tests," Emily said, "don't allow for the way America's Blacks have been socialized for generations."

"Why then aren't there prosperous Negro societies in Africa? Why do people there have to be periodically rescued from famine? Why is Haiti—which has the highest percentage of Blacks in the Western Hemisphere—the poorest, most ungovernable country in the Americas?

"The possibility that Blacks are genetically inferior would be under consideration if we were talking about breeds of dogs rather than human beings."

"There are other factors at work," Emily said. "In much of this hemisphere educating Blacks has been illegal for hundreds of years. Their schools are still inferior.

"Worse yet, they're seldom raised by both parents because slavery destroyed the Black family. Mothers, fathers, sons, and daughters were sold to different owners—never to see each other again. Like cattle, females were bred every year to their owners or to males chosen by their owners. So they learned to have numerous babies, starting at young ages.

People react to the humiliation of racism by becoming passive or by becoming enraged and indulging in activities not in their best interests, such as drug abuse or alcoholism. Sadly, they often lash out violently toward others of their race.

"After emancipation, most Black men knew nothing but farming and became sharecroppers. Plantation owners gave them land to work and a percentage of the profits on their crops.

"Company stores encouraged them to spend more than they had, so they'd be in debt and couldn't leave. If today's Blacks spend money recklessly, it's because that's what generations of their forebears were taught."

"You wouldn't," Larry said, consciously avoiding an argumentative tone, "let a White man excuse his failings by pointing to abuses suffered generations ago."

"It wasn't that long ago," Emily said, sitting up. "When Blacks went to work in armaments factories during World War II, many had never seen U.S. currency because plantations issued their own private money, forcing sharecroppers to spend their earnings in company stores.

"When the NAACP convinced the Supreme Court to desegregate America's schools, the most telling argument was a study by Kenneth and Mamie Clark. In numerous parts of the country, they'd shown young Black girls dolls that were identical, except for the color of their skin, hair, and eyes.

"Asked to choose the doll that looked most like them, the girls pointed to the Black doll. Asked to pick the most beautiful doll, they selected the ones with pink skin, blue eyes, and blond hair. Discrimination, and segregation had produced a sense of inferiority and self-hatred.

"That finding convinced the Supreme Court to order the integration of America's schools."

"What is it you want to talk about?" Larry asked, softly touching his wife's arm.

"Last night," Emily replied, "the counselor at New Beginnings told me it may take a long time to find us another newborn White baby. He asked if we'd consider a Black child."

"That's strange," Larry said. "He told me it's their policy to place Black children with Black parents."

"They've reconsidered. There are too many Blacks up for adoption these days."

"I don't see any reason why we can't adopt a Black baby," Larry said, "but I'd prefer that child to be a newborn."

"So would I."

—∞—

Emily's family had immigrated from Russia. During their Orthodox wedding ceremony, she and Larry had each lighted a candle. Custom dictated that the one whose candle was held higher would have the upper hand in their marriage.

Their guests had expected two such high-powered individuals to stand on tiptoes, if not chairs. But no matter how low Emily held her candle, Larry's was lower until both were on the floor. Their families saw this as a sign they'd have a happy marriage.

—∞—

At that morning's meeting of the Commission, Gene Rice summed up his previous day's presentation.

"No group in America," he began, "has Blacks' unanimity of opinion. Nearly ninety percent identify as Democrats and believe Whites are obligated to help solve their problems. I'm called a traitor to my race because I disagree."

Avery King scrambled to his feet, and Larry braced for an explosion.

"Mr. Chairman," King said, unexpectedly calm, "I'd like to hear from a person well-qualified to refute Mr. Rice's misrepresentations."

"Do you have someone in mind?" Larry asked.

"Emily Winslow," King said, looking at her, eyebrows raised.

Emily stood hesitantly, then strode to the podium. Larry had no idea what she'd say.

"White people," she began, "were infuriated when Malcolm X, a prominent Black Muslim, called President John Kennedy's assassination 'a case of chickens coming home to roost.' Yet uncounted thousands of Caucasians publicly rejoiced over Martin Luther King's assassination.

"That's a diplomatic way of saying some Whites and some Blacks are to blame for America's racial woes. And that was progress of a sort because prior to emancipation, White slave owners were 100% in the wrong. And during the Jim Crow era, White racists were 100% at fault.

"In those days, Black men and women shared a single segregated restroom, usually bypassed by the janitor. They drank from 'Coloreds only' water fountains. They rode in the backs of buses, and drivers would order an entire row to stand if one White person needed a seat.

"The Montgomery Bus Boycott was sparked when Rosa Parks, a middle-aged Black woman, refused to give her seat to a White man.

"Whites consider Black violence inexcusable, forgetting that there was a time when—if White Southern Judges ruled in favor of Blacks—they had to be guarded day and night by federal marshals.

"The murders of Black activists in the South went unnoticed until White civil rights workers suffered the same fate.

"For years Blacks were entitled to vote and serve on juries, but were prevented from exercising those rights. They were also forced to take the worst jobs.

"Competition with the Soviet Union during the Cold War forced an end to many of these abuses—not because it was right, but because America wanted allies in the event of a hot war.

"When Whites protested the O.J. Simpson decision—which set a murderer free—they conveniently forgot their own use of jury nullification to acquit Caucasians guilty of crimes against Blacks and to convict innocent Negroes."

"But today—in the modern Civil Rights era—we see Blacks who are their own worst enemies and can justifiably be called upon to make the changes that Mr. Rice calls for."

Emily thanked her audience, then sat down. She'd managed to speak her mind without saying anything that would put her at odds with Larry. But serving on the Commission would get more difficult unless she resigned.

CHAPTER THIRTEEN
IF MARTIN LUTHER KING ONLY KNEW

FOLLOWING THE Koreatown incident, Governor Webster hastily returned from Japan. Within an hour of landing in Los Angeles, he summoned city officials and civic leaders—including Avery King—to a Summit Conference.

King's visit to Iran after the Shah fled Ayatollah Khomeini's revolution had made him a pariah. He claimed to be visiting his son, who was attending the University of Tehran. Photos of him shaking hands with students who'd taken four hundred American hostages at the U.S. Embassy had ignited a firestorm of protest.

Never one to shy away from publicity, King convinced the Governor they should show their concern about the Koreatown incident. Within the hour Webster announced what he called a Goodwill Tour of South Central. He was answering reporters' questions when Brian Waterman left the room to call KTLA and change the lead story on his nightly broadcast.

At home that evening, Ted Roffman watched Webster's press conference on television. Every time he growled, his black Lab, Mogul, stood up and left the room.

"Summit Conference and Goodwill Tour," he shouted at his television set, "are fancy titles for riding around in bulletproof cars with enough cops to provoke a riot."

The following day, Larry and Ted Roffman met with a police sergeant. Together, the three searched for Blacks who—on television—had begged the Guard to stay longer in South Central after the Watts and Rodney King Riots.

The day after that, Larry flew to Los Angeles with Don Maxwell, his bodyguard, and the list of people he wanted to interview. He started with Dexter Allen.

"While the Guard was here," Allen told Larry, "my wife and I could safely walk to stores, which we'd never done before. By the time I had enough signatures on a petition asking the Guard to stay, they were already evacuating the area.

"People living in New Orleans after Hurricane Katrina also pleaded with the Guard to stay after looting, arson, and sniping broke out. Of fifteen thousand soldiers sent to restore order, some four hundred were left behind to help the police."

Larry's other interviews had been equally unproductive when he and Don met with the last person on his list.

Kathleen Mitchell welcomed Larry into her home and served cookies and milk at her chrome and Formica kitchen table.

Well-educated, she still resembled the woman who—thirty-eight years earlier—had begged on her knees for the Guard to stay and had accurately predicted that one of her sons, Billy, would soon be dead if the soldiers left.

Eloquently she told Larry, "When my boys were young, I placed their feet on the right path, but when the eldest was older, bigger, and stronger, he chose a path that led to the Bloods. When I asked why, he said that was the only way he could protect himself from the gangs.

"Not long after the Guard pulled out, the Crips shot and killed him. A police sergeant brought me the news and said LAPD had no leads. They didn't even know if my boy was the intended target. Gang members aren't sharpshooters. They spray bullets and hope.

"South Central is an upside down world where mothers bury their sons rather than the other way around. I teamed up with other single mothers, and we moved our families to Palmdale—sixty-two miles north of Los Angeles—where we'd been told there were no gangs.

"While looking for local employment we carpooled to our old jobs, a four-hour round-trip. Unbeknownst to us, some of our kids were already gang members, and they brought that sickness with them. Six months later the police brought the news. My Billy had been murdered during the funeral and burial of a fellow Blood in Palmdale."

The old lady closed her dark, sad eyes and covered her face with both hands, hiding tears she couldn't hold back.

"What would I have to do," Larry asked, "to get you to tell your story to the Governor's Commission on South Central?"

"Just ask me," she said. "I want to help. Only the National Guard has ever shut the gangs down, and if they come back I want them to stay long enough to do the job permanently."

"That was heartbreaking," Don said when he and Larry were back in their rental car. "That poor woman lost both her boys even though she made a superhuman effort to keep them alive."

"If the National Guard had stayed in South Central after the Rodney King Riot," Larry said, "her sons would still be alive."

"Theoretically," Don replied, "but the Commission will never recommend leaving the Guard that long and Governor Webster won't implement it if they do.

"By the way, I did some research on the internet. Dexter Allen was wrong. New Orleans wasn't the only city where the Guard stayed for an extended period. Back in the '60s, Governor Charles Terry left troops in Wilmington, Delaware for nearly ten months. The resulting ruckus cost Terry his office and almost his life.

"He reportedly ordered the Guard to shoot looters but their Commander refused. Order was quickly restored, but the Guard was still there when Terry ran for re-election months later. His lead in the polls was comfortable when a heart attack stopped him from campaigning. He barely lost.

"The new governor's first official act was to withdraw the troops. Terry had appointed more Blacks to state posts than any Delaware governor before him, but he'll be remembered as a racist. Are you sure you want to go down that same road?"

During the drive to their hotel, Larry saw a small child standing on the curb in a freshly-ironed dress, crying.

"Pull over," he said.

Maxwell stopped beside the girl and turned off the motor.

Larry opened the door and stepped out. Looking at houses on both sides of the street, he wondered if someone watching would object to his approaching a little girl.

"Are you a pohlicemun?" the girl asked, shrinking from him. "I'm scared of pohlicemuns."

At her age, Larry had seen policemen as protectors.

"I'm not a police officer," he said, squatting. "They wear uniforms."

"How come you got that Black man locked up in your car?"

"He's not locked up. He's my friend."

Larry beckoned. Don got out of the car, knelt and asked. "What's your name?"

"Tamika," the girl replied. "My brother says gonna be a war with the police. I wanna go home, but I'm lost."

Larry stood and faced an elderly Black man behind them.

"Marion Camby," the man introduced himself. "May I ask your name?"

"Larry Winslow. Is this your daughter?"

"No, but when my wife and I go for walks, we often see her playing. She lives around that corner."

"Do you know this man," Larry asked.

"Not really," Tamika said.

"We live in a suspicious world," Camby said sadly. "Tamika doesn't trust any of us. I came out here to protect her from you, and now you wonder if you can trust me. My wife," he pointed to a lady coming out of the house behind them, "will make sure she gets home."

Mrs. Camby picked up Tamika, who relaxed against her as if she no longer had a shape of her own.

Back in the rental car after Tamika was safely home, Don glanced at his wrist watch.

"Let's go to Carl Young's speech tonight," he suggested, "Kathleen Mitchell gave me tickets. We can get there in plenty of time."

—m—

Reverend Carl Young was America's most prominent living civil rights leader. He'd started as an assistant to Martin Luther King. Unlike many of that great man's followers,

Young had remained loyal when King's strategy of nonviolence was swept aside by Black Panthers and big city riots.

Two days after the Watts riot, King and his staff had gone there. Later Young reported that his heart broke and never healed when activists ridiculed King and brushed him aside.

After King's assassination, Young confronted racism with boycotts, court cases, and demonstrations. He was unique in that he also spoke out when he thought Blacks were in the wrong, such as when they advocated teaching ebonics (ebony phonics) in public school.

Young had scheduled tonight's speech in a poor neighborhood. All day, volunteers had handed out free tickets door-to-door.

When Larry and Don arrived, the huge revival tent was packed. They found seats high in the bleachers as Carl Young came on stage.

"South Central is near the boiling point," Young began his trademark chant. "Once again, committees and commissions are looking at the Black Problem instead of the White Problem. For European-Americans to be cured of the sickness known as racism, they must be taught to see us in a way that doesn't reinforce their prejudices.

"Riots don't show us as we are, and they're wasteful. They *waste* lives. They *waste* our talents as well as the inventions, books, paintings, and much more we have inside, waiting to be shared."

At first Larry listened with his mind, then with his heart. Finally he stopped listening. Sadly, he remembered how police work had changed him. Carl Young's words made him wish he'd tried harder.

After his speech, Young shook hands with people who'd lined up to thank him. For an hour, Larry and Don sat in the bleachers watching him greet well-wishers as if there was nothing he'd rather be doing.

"I'm going to congratulate the Reverend on his speech," Don said. "Why don't you join me? You can ask what he thinks about leaving the Guard in South Central for a couple of years."

"I think I'll thank him for coming and leave it at that," Larry said, grinning.

As they stood in the reception line, Larry's eyes never left Carl Young.

—m—

Muhammad Nasheed, too, was studying Carl Young. He'd idolized the man before realizing his policy of non-violence did more harm than good. The time had come. Young could now accomplish more by dying than living.

He'd be the ideal martyr. Whites would be blamed for his murder, and Blacks would be enraged. He'd go down in history as America's most famous sacrificial lamb since Martin Luther King.

—m—

As Larry waited for his moment with Carl Young, he wondered if the man sometimes wished he could speak his mind without worrying about how the media would spin his message. When Larry's turn came, he thanked the reverend for helping in Los Angeles's hour of need.

"You're Larry Winslow, the Lieutenant Governor, aren't you?" Young asked, prolonging their handshake.

Larry nodded.

"My foundation," Young continued, "bought stock in your company back when it was up and coming and you were a boy wonder. Best investment we ever made."

Standing at a polite distance, Young's aides looked impatient. They'd been waiting for their share of his time since his speech ended.

"How," Young asked Larry, "did an obviously prosperous White man get a ticket for tonight? Those were earmarked exclusively for South Central residents. No matter. I'm glad you came.

"Horace Grayson told me about your work on the Governor's South Central Commission. He called you 'a rare politician who avoids the limelight.' He also told me you tend to blame Blacks for their problems."

"Some Blacks for some of their problems," Larry corrected. "I think it's fair to say the Governor's Commission has spent most of its time on the White Problem. But the more we meet and talk, the more confused I get."

"That's a good sign. How does the saying go?" Young paused. "'In this day and age, if you're not confused, perhaps you don't understand the situation.'"

"How do you think Martin Luther King would react," Larry asked, "if he knew what's happened since his murder?"

"I think it would break his heart," Young replied as one of his aides placed a hand on his shoulder and whispered something.

"I hope we meet again soon," Young told Larry. "I'd like to know you better."

Watching Young walk away, Larry realized he should've invited Young to address the Commission.

CHAPTER FOURTEEN
WASTE! WASTE! WASTE!

LEWIS FRANKLIN had spent the day interviewing people in South Central for his next book. At midnight, after a productive day, he got into his rental car and started for his hotel. Waiting at a stoplight, he watched a young Black man trying to flag down a taxi.

Two passed, the drivers pretending they hadn't seen him. Before the American Civil Liberties Union successfully sued two cab companies, they'd explained this with stories of young Black men robbing drivers, or worse. Now they denied rather than justified that policy.

Franklin drove around the block, stopped beside the young man, and opened his front passenger door.

"Where you headed?" he asked.

"Ovah neah Alameda 'n Imperial."

"I'll be happy to take you," Franklin said. "It's not far out of my way."

The young man slid inside, fumbling with his loose-fitting sweatshirt. After pulling into traffic, Franklin's attempts to start a conversation fell flat, and he was reminded of something Jessie Jackson had said.

"There is nothing more painful to me," the civil rights leader had told an interviewer, "than to walk down the street and hear footsteps and start thinking about robbery, then look around and see somebody White and feel relieved."

"Tuhn raht at the next conah," the young man ordered.

A pistol pointed at his belly, Franklin turned onto a dark street.

"Is this how you repay me?" he asked.

"Will you hand ovah yo' monah if I asks all nice and polite? Stop, and gimme yo' wallet. Then ah gets out, and you drives away. I ain't gonna hurt ya unless you does something stoopid."

Later in his hotel room, Franklin decided not to file a police report. Soon the Governor's Commission would decide whether to recommend responding to a riot by sending the Guard to South Central. He didn't want his misfortune to become an argument in favor of Larry Winslow's racist proposal to leave them there indefinitely.

The next morning, the *Los Angeles Times* had six-inch headlines. Carl Young had been assassinated by a sniper. An LAPD forensics specialist had determined the bullet was armor-piercing and had passed through Mr. Young's upper body and the armored car doors on either side of him. It was fired while his vehicle was passing a vacant lot.

This news hit the Black community hard. Young's spokesman, Calvin Wilson, asked for restraint.

"If you demand an eye for an eye and a tooth for a tooth," he quoted Martin Luther King, "you wind up with everyone blind and toothless."

Lewis Franklin changed his mind, and told viewers on KTLA: "Last night, I was robbed at gunpoint by a man who happened to be Black. If Reverend Young's assassin was White, that murder can't be held against all Whites any more than all Blacks are guilty of stealing my money."

—᠁—

When Young's assassination didn't ignite the feared riot, Governor Webster went ahead with his Koreatown visit. His armored limousine was escorted by motorcycle patrolmen with pistol-grip shotguns in scabbards.

Near an intersection with grocery stores on three of four corners, the motorcade came upon hundreds of shoppers. They were hoarding food to tide them over in the event of a riot. The crush of cars and pedestrians brought traffic to a standstill.

—᠁—

Muhammad Nasheed watched the motorcade drive into his trap. After personally shooting Carl Young, he'd waited for South Central to explode. When it hadn't, his father had convinced the Governor to go ahead with his Goodwill Tour.

LAPD had been tight-lipped about the motorcade's route, but a Muslim patrolman had gotten it for him. When panic buying broke out that morning, he'd selected an intersection where gridlock was inevitable and the motorcade would be delayed.

That morning, Nasheed's father had conveniently gotten sick and excused himself from the motorcade.

"There's no need for restraint," Nasheed told his lieutenants before sending them into the crowd to provoke the riot he'd planned for months.

—᠁—

Private security guards were letting shoppers into the packed stores only after others came out. Those waiting outside filled the sidewalks and overflowed into the streets.

They were worried the stores would be sold out before they got in, and tempers were short.

Men surrounded the Governor's limousine with well-rehearsed precision. Shoppers in line moving closer to the stores' entrances abruptly joined what seemed to be a spontaneous event. With the Governor's vehicle isolated in their midst they began angrily chanting: "Waste! Waste! Waste!" Pause. "Waste! Waste! Waste!", describing Carl Young's murder with his words.

The tightly packed crowd blocked other policemen from coming to the motorcycle escort's aid. The escorts dismounted, lowered their kickstands, and stood next to their shotguns.

"We need help *now*," the officer in charge barked into his radio.

"Coming," was the terse reply. "People are blocking us on purpose."

"Waste! Waste! Waste!" Pause. "Waste! Waste! Waste!"

—m—

The chant drowned out the sound of rocks and bottles hitting the limousines. Carl Young's aide, Calvin Wilson, stepped out of the Governor's vehicle. Hit by a thrown rock, he ducked back inside and locked the door.

"Reverend Young," he told Webster, "could've handled this."

"Avery King, too," Governor Webster added. "This was a damned inconvenient time for him to get sick."

Ignoring commands to stay back, people cupped their hands against the limousine's tinted windows and peered inside, taunting the occupants.

"Blacks," Calvin Wilson said, "have never assassinated a governor—not even George Wallace. A White man fired the bullet that paralyzed him."

Several men poured water into a planter box, then coated the limousine's windows with mud. As a group rocked the car, the motorcycle patrolmen drew their eight gauge shotguns.

Blocks away, LAPD positioned barricades so vehicles could leave—but not enter—the area. Police reinforcements forced their way through the tightly packed crowd.

"Let's hold Webster hostage," someone proposed, "until the FBI finds Carl Young's assassin. That'll give them incentive."

After removing his shirt, a man began cleaning the mud-smeared windshield.

"Get your Black ass away from that vehicle," another man ordered, brandishing a pistol. Ignoring him, the shirtless man organized a group to clear a path through the crowd, then the limousine slowly proceeded under a hail of rocks and bottles.

Beyond the intersection, squad cars with flashing lights and screaming sirens surrounded the limousine. Then it raced past the speed limit and kept accelerating.

—∞—

The International Airport's futuristic Encounter Restaurant was a Los Angeles landmark. Its flying-saucer-shaped dining area sat high in the air atop a circular elevator shaft. It was further supported by a pair of intersecting arches and featured space age decor and a spectacular 360 degree view.

The background noise and conversations faded as television news programs gave viewers the latest details on the investigation of Carl Young's murder.

Larry Winslow and Don Maxwell had finished breakfast when the latter's cell phone rang and he stepped away to talk in private.

"Governor Webster was shot," he explained after returning. "I have to go to St. Vincent's Hospital in South Central to protect him."

As Maxwell rushed toward the elevator, Larry set his cup on the table and waved off the waiter coming to refill it. He'd have to fly to Sacramento without a bodyguard. No problem. People wouldn't recognize him. No one ever did.

—∞—

In the plane's aisle, waiting to disembark in Sacramento, Larry called Emily.

"Thank God," she said, answering on the first ring. "Where are you?"

"Sacramento airport," he replied. "I got out of L.A. just before the mother of all riots."

"I'm worried about you. Please be careful."

"I will. Love you."

Inside the terminal, people were gathered around TV screens watching CNN's coverage of the so-called Carl Young Riot. Governor Webster's bodyguard, the one called Darth Vader, was waiting.

Tall, muscular, and constantly alert, Vader scanned the crowd. Seeing something he didn't like, he grabbed Larry's arm with a huge hand, then guided him to a door and entered the code to open it. Once inside, he shut the door and stood with his back pressed against it.

"When I heard Don Maxwell is standing guard in Governor Webster's hospital room," he told Larry, "I figured he was protecting my man so I'd look after his."

"Hospital room." Larry frowned. "What happened?"

"Governor Webster's motorcade was attacked by a mob and he was shot. He's on the critical list. When you get to your office you'll be sworn in as acting governor."

Larry's chest tightened. A month earlier, he'd felt unqualified to lead a discussion about a possible riot. Now he had to handle what was potentially the worst ever.

Events hadn't gone as Muhammad Nasheed planned, but he had his riot. LAPD had activated every man it had. Soon there would be thousands of officers in South Central, all potential targets.

The moment Nasheed had worked for had come, and he was ready.

CHAPTER FIFTEEN
MARTIAL LAW

DURING THE drive to his office, Larry called Emily again.

"Did you hear that Governor Webster was shot?" he asked.

"CNN just corrected their initial report," Emily replied. "He wasn't shot. He suffered a massive heart attack."

"I'm about to be sworn in as acting governor," Larry told her. "Hope I'm up to the job."

"You will be," she assured him. "You're outstanding in a crisis."

Governor Webster's chief of staff, Bob Pickering, was waiting in Larry's office with the Chief Justice of California's Supreme Court. The oath of office was administered using a Bible bound in white morocco leather with gold lettering.

"If I can help with anything," Pickering offered after the swearing-in, "all you have to do is ask."

Befitting Larry's new status, the atmosphere of his office changed abruptly. The phone rang until every light on the receptionist's console was lit. Fax machines churned out paper as if they were printing presses. Computers chirped as email came in.

Unnoticed in the hubbub, Darth Vader sat in the lobby, staring over the top of an open magazine, watching people come and go.

After the expected call from Los Angeles Mayor Dean Payne, Larry dialed General Nelson's direct number at California National Guard Headquarters.

"As acting governor," he began after Nelson answered, "I've been notified that the mayor of Los Angeles wants CANG troops as soon as possible. I'll issue an executive order authorizing you to use as many troops and armored personnel carriers as necessary to minimize the loss of life. May I put you on speaker phone? I'd like my aides to hear our conversation."

Nelson waited, asked if everyone could hear him, then said, "There's rioting along a thirty-two mile stretch from the Hollywood Hills to Long Beach. To put a lid on an area that big, we'll need help from the Marines."

"I'll arrange for that," Larry said. "I also want to address the troops before they go in."

"Their officers will take care of that," Nelson replied curtly.

"I insist."

Shaking his fist, Ted mouthed the words, "Atta boy."

"In that case," Nelson said crisply, "you can fly to Los Angeles with me and address the troops that are there. We'll broadcast your speech to the rest. My aide, Tony Jackson—you met him last week—will meet you at Mather Air Force Base's main gate. Don't be late. I leave at five sharp."

"How soon can you have troops in the riot area?"

"Ten hours at best," Nelson said. "It takes time to pull people off their jobs, then equip and transport them."

"Are you sure," Bridges asked after Larry hung up, "you should give the general a blank check on the number of armored personnel carriers he can deploy? That will get you criticized for using excessive force."

"I want to stop this riot before it gains momentum," Larry said. "I've also arranged for the L. A. County Sheriff, the Commander of the California Highway Patrol, and the Marines to send all the men they can."

Lois Brady poked her head into Larry's office.

"I've typed your Declaration of Martial Law," she said. "What should I do with it?"

"Avery King," Ted Roffman groused, closing Larry's office door behind himself, "couldn't manage to go to South Central with Governor Webster, but has courageously left his sick bed to tell you how to run things."

Larry's shoulders drooped as he said, "Show him in. We might as well get past this now."

Halfway through the door King huffed, "If you put the Guard in South Central for an extended period. I'll fight you tooth and nail."

Larry made no attempt to hide his sigh.

"Glad you're feeling better," he told King.

"I just heard that you declared martial law. A state of emergency would've been sufficient."

"Martial law suspends certain civil rights," Larry said, "which a state of emergency leaves in effect. If past riots are an indication, those rights make it exceedingly difficult to restore order."

"How do you think South Central's peaceful residents will feel about having their civil rights suspended, even though they're doing nothing illegal? I—"

"Avery, I don't have time for this. I've made up my mind."

"See you in court," King barked, charging out the door.

Larry waved Michael Bridges into his office.

"Remember that television footage of Reginald Denny being beaten during the Rodney King Riot? I need a copy to show the troops before they go into the riot area."

"Jesus." Michael winced. "Are you sure you want them to see *that*? It could put them in the wrong frame of mind."

"Not if I call their attention to the important details." Larry dialed his phone.

Again Emily answered on the first ring.

"I'm going to Los Angeles this afternoon," he told her, "and may be there several days. Can you fly down and meet with me there? I have to make some quick decisions, and your input would be very helpful. You won't get parked in a hotel room. Where I go, you'll go—unless it's not safe."

"I'll email you my flight itinerary."

"Don't fly to Los Angeles International. People are shooting at planes landing there. I'll have someone pick you up at the Orange County airport."

Larry hurried down the hall to Roffman's office. Ted's assistant, Camille Bryant, was crying.

"I'm okay," she told him. "Tonight's first news reports said Governor Webster had been shot. My reaction was the same as when I heard President Kennedy had been shot in Dallas. I prayed the shooter wasn't Black."

"I understand," Larry said. "I don't want it to be a White person who shot Carl Young."

"I can't think of another reasonable possibility. Can you?"

"Not at the moment."

The Los Angeles Coliseum had hosted the track-and field-events at the Olympic Games in 1932 and 1984. Now it was a staging area for California's National Guard. Soldiers had reported to nearby armories and been trucked in from there. Standing on the playing field, surrounded by a hundred thousand empty seats, they seemed pitifully few.

"They'll be the tip of the spear," General Nelson told Larry. "We'll deploy a total of eighteen thousand troops within twenty-four hours. During riots, the law requires we convert our rifles from full to semi-automatic, to prevent guardsmen from spraying bullets into crowds.

"Unfortunately, the lock plates and installers were delayed. The longer we wait, the more dangerous the situation becomes. I've decided to send my men in now. To comply with the law, they won't have clips and will have to reload after every shot. God help 'em if they come up against gangs with automatic weapons."

The general led the way up a short flight of stairs to a platform. Using the microphone there, he ordered the troops to gather around.

"My men at Camp Pendleton and other staging areas," he told Larry, "will see and hear you on a remote feed."

"The most enduring images of the Rodney King Riot," Larry began, "were shot from a helicopter with a telephoto lens. They show a White truck driver, Reginald Denny, being savagely beaten by Black gang members."

The video on a large screen behind Larry showed a semi-truck, its windshield smashed. Attackers forced the door and pulled the driver out. While Denny was face down, one stepped on his head while a companion repeatedly kicked him.

Someone hit him with a hammer. Someone else heaved a chunk of concrete at his head leaving him motionless while another man danced on his body, laughing and flashing gang signs.

"Unfortunately," Larry continued, "the helicopter was fired on and left the area. That's truly a shame because the nationwide audience missed what happened next.

"After watching a rerun of the attack on television, a Black truck driver, Bobby Green, and three friends rushed to the intersection. Denny was drifting in and out of consciousness, attempting to drive away, and gang members were screaming, 'Finish him off.'

"Green climbed into Denny's truck and eased him out of the driver's seat. Unable to see through the shattered windshield, he drove to the nearest hospital while a companion cradled Denny in her arms and their two friends led the way in a car.

"Denny had a seizure in the emergency room and nearly died. His skull was fractured in countless places and pressing against his brain. One eye was so badly dislocated that doctors feared it would fall into his sinus cavity.

"The doctors who saved Reginald Denny's life were Black. Four Blacks had put his life in danger, but six others saved him. Please remember, not everyone you see tonight will be a looter, arsonist, or gang member."

The video on the screen was replaced by an enlargement of a photo Emily brought with her from Sacramento. It showed a Black man in a chair on a sidewalk, a shotgun across his thighs. He was dark-skinned with flaring nostrils and full lips. Race-baiters call his kind *"gorillas."*

"This man's name," Larry continued, "is Roscoe O'Neill. During the Rodney King Riot, the Guard didn't reach his neighborhood for days. While waiting, he ate, slept, and sat in that chair, protecting the store behind him. He and its White owner were friends.

"In my worst nightmare, a guardsman shot him dead when he didn't raise his hands as ordered. Thank God, the Guard simply disarmed him and sent him home.

"In days to come, you may be forced to use your weapons. If this is like past riots, however, residents will come out of their homes to thank you. Store owners will refuse your money when you try to pay for merchandise. Restaurants will give you free meals. And school children will send thank-you notes after you leave."

"That was beautiful," Emily greeted as Larry trotted down the stairs from the stage. "Your little refresher was a timely reminder of the important fact that these men will be dealing with people who—above all—are human beings."

Larry, Emily, and General Nelson watched as trucks returned from the riot area to pick up more guardsmen.

"When can you let reporters in?" Larry asked.

"When the situation is under control," Nelson replied, "and there's no danger they'll reveal information that tells looters where the action is."

"General," Emily said, "may I please speak with the acting Governor for a moment?"

"Are you sure you want to do that?" Emily asked as Nelson walked away. "Freedom of the Press is protected by the Constitution."

"It can legally be suspended," Larry said, "under martial law."

"Doing that will give the impression you're hiding something. Is there a less controversial way to keep the media from inadvertently making these men's mission more difficult?"

"When you ask questions like that," Larry shook his scolding finger playfully, "it means you have a suggestion. Out with it."

"Rather than lock reporters out, you could ban satellite trucks and prohibit live broadcasts. That allows the media to inform the public when things quiet down. The best defense against charges of excessive force is to have the media film what's happening."

"That," Larry said, "is the sort of input I anticipated when I asked you to come with me tonight."

After Larry explained his decision, Nelson testily asked, "Are you ordering me to let the press in?"

"I prefer to make it a suggestion," Larry replied.

"I'd rather have an order in writing to cover my ass."

"Coming up." Larry took a smartphone from his briefcase.

CHAPTER SIXTEEN
THE VICTIM MENTALITY

AS THE first armored vehicles left for the riot area, Larry asked Nelson, "How will you announce tomorrow's curfew?"

"The usual. Posters. The media. Loudspeaker trucks."

"Can you send troop trucks to help people get to work until public transportation is restored? That'll bring the Guard much-needed goodwill."

"Along with a ton of liability," Nelson said firmly. "It's difficult to sue the military, but if civilians are injured in our trucks, lawyers will find a way. If you want me to take that risk, you'll have to order me in writing, and I'll need time to work out the details."

"Tony Jackson already did that." Larry handed Nelson a folder. "He's working on his Young People's Project now."

"The legislature will never fund the Young People's Project," Nelson scoffed. "They'll see it as rewarding rioters."

"I'll raise the money from private sources."

Grinning, Nelson clicked his heels, saluted, and said, "I'm a bit of a frustrated social engineer, itching to make the real world as orderly as ours. That's why I plan to have my troops bivouac in South Central's parks and schoolyards, where they can associate with the residents and be immediately available to protect and help them.

—꧂—

On the way to a hotel, their driver, Bill Pope, took Emily and Larry around the riot area.

"Can we get closer?" Larry asked. "All I can see from here is the glow of distant fires."

"I'd like a better view myself," Pope said. "But I have orders to avoid areas where there's rioting. Gene Rice is taking calls from eyewitnesses on his radio show. Would you like to listen?"

"That would be helpful," Larry said.

At an interchange where their freeway passed above others, traffic came to a standstill, and Larry heard screaming sirens. As far as he could see, orange-red flames boiled from buildings, gushing acrid smoke.

Pope turned Gene Rice's program off, then back on.

"I was hoping," he explained, "that gunfire was on the radio but it's nearby."

"We have better things than this to do in Sacramento," Larry said. "Please take us to the airport."

"LA International is closed, but you can catch a military flight. I'll radio ahead and make arrangements."

Again Larry realized how unprepared he was for his new job. A Private in the National Guard knew more about a governor's powers than he did.

Pope contacted Los Angeles Air Force Base on his two-way radio, then persistently worked his way up the chain of command until he got an answer he liked.

"There's an Air Force flight tonight," he told Larry. "They'll hold it for you, but only briefly." He programmed his vehicle's GPS for the fastest route to the L.A. Air Force Base.

"Bill," Larry said, "you get things done and I have a lot to do. How would you like to work for me on the Young People's Project?"

"I read about it," Pope said. "Sounds like something I'd enjoy."

"It involves long hours," Larry cautioned. "Are you married?"

"Nope. I'm footloose and fancy free. When can I start?"

"Right now."

"Where were you staying in Los Angeles?" Pope asked.

"The downtown Marriott."

"Give me your room keys. I'll check you out and bring your suitcases when I come to Sacramento. Where shall I meet you?"

As gridlock became stop-and-go traffic, Emily slid closer to Larry and whispered, "Hiring him was an excellent idea. He's a self-starter with a fast mind and a good heart."

CHAPTER SEVENTEEN
A DOMESTIC VIETNAM

DURING THE riot's early hours, nine of LAPD's beleaguered officers and an equal number of soldiers were murdered by snipers. Then the shooting stopped. By morning order had restored itself more than been restored.

The next day's news was top-heavy with inexplicable happenings.

A looter, his car stuffed with booty, had been seen speeding down an abandoned street, obediently coming to a complete stop at every traffic light and stop sign.

A White teacher, John Jessup—fleeing South Central—stopped at a red light and saw a man with a Molotov cocktail trying to ignite its wick. Jessup raised his handgun. Seeing its laser sight's red dot on his shirt, the man ambled away with a friendly wave while Jessup vomited in his car.

A sergeant in charge of guardsmen behind a barricade of sawhorses spotted Deshawn Jefferson, a Black man, staggering toward them with a bottle. The Sergeant watched him pull a match from a book of them and light it. It flickered out. Ignoring commands to stop, Jefferson lit another.

Rifle to his shoulder, a soldier asked, "Shall I shoot before he gets close enough to throw that Molotov cocktail?"

"Hold your fire," the Sergeant bellowed. "He has an unlit cigarette in his mouth."

The Sergeant approached Jefferson cautiously—rifle at the ready—and took his bottle away. Empty, it smelled of whiskey.

—∾—

Tom Jensen, a White LAPD officer, surprised a Black boy out after curfew and took him by the arm.

"It's your choice, son," he said gently. "You can go home or to jail."

"I'm not your fucking son," the boy snarled, yanking a pistol from behind his belt and backing away.

Somehow, Jensen resisted the urge to draw his sidearm while another officer snuck up behind the boy and put him in an arm hold that forced the revolver from his hand. It wasn't loaded.

—∾—

In another incident two LAPD officers—supported by marines—knocked on a door and a shotgun blast was fired through it, wounding one.

"Cover me," the other yelled.

The marines fired numerous rounds into the house, killing a man and a woman."I didn't mean for them to do that," the officer later told reporters. "To a policeman, 'cover me' means be ready."

"To us," one of the marines explained, "it means lay down cover fire at once."

—⁂—

In a residential area, a National Guard patrol came upon a boy standing near a curb up to his knees in leaves he'd raked.

"What for you soldiers driving 'round heah in Humvees?" he asked, eyes wide.

"Well," Sergeant Matthew Lupo said, stepping out of his vehicle, "we don't have any Cadillacs."

"Us poor folks, neither." Quick on the uptake, the boy chuckled.

"What's your name?" Lupo asked.

"Steven Shell."

"It's not safe to be outside, Steven. I'll walk you home. Where do you live?"

The boy pointed to a house with curtains flapping in open windows.

"Who takes care of you?" Lupo asked.

"My sister. My dad's dead, and my mom's at work."

"Why aren't you hiding like everyone else?"

"I'm not afraid of soldiers. I'm gonna be one someday."

A teenage girl—clearly apprehensive—held the screen door open.

"This is a promise." Sergeant Lupo crossed his heart. "If you and Steven promise to stay in your house until there's no longer a curfew, I'll bring you enough hamburgers and hot dogs for the rest of the week."

Pointing, the girl said, "There's a McDonalds over there."

"It's closed," Lupo told her, "but I know one that isn't."

With no further explanation, Lupo and his patrol drove away. Later they returned with handfuls of plump McDonald's bags.

"We also brought enough for your mom," Lupo explained, smiling.

Muhammad Nasheed's men were no match for the soldiers and armored vehicles of the National Guard. He'd expected residents to rise up and overwhelm their common enemy. But with most locals on the sidelines, the Guard had quickly restored order.

With the soldiers bivouacked in parks throughout South Central, the wily Nasheed called off his men, his version of the proverbial step backward in order to continue forward later. Immediately he started work on a new plan. By the time he executed it, he'd know everything there was to know about Acting Governor Winslow, a very different opponent from the one he'd anticipated.

CHAPTER EIGHTEEN
OARS IN THE WATER

The psychological impact of armored personnel carriers had been amplified by removing their mufflers. Time and again, roaring engines, clanking treads, and loudspeakers had announced their arrival before Nasheed's men could massacre outnumbered policemen they'd boxed in.

The APC's, however, became a two-edged sword the next morning. Their photos were on the front pages of the world's newspapers. America's friends praised their crews' skill and restraint. Her enemies compared them to the tanks with which the USSR brutally crushed the 1956 Hungarian Revolution.

The following morning, civilians at South Central's bus stops were picked up by National Guard trucks and taken to where public transportation was available. Early on Manchester Avenue, one stopped for its first passengers and a young White Private helped them aboard, then sat in front with the driver.

"That was reassuring," the Private whispered. "Blacks aren't all natural athletes."

"Not all Whites are natural scholars either," the driver—a Black Sergeant—said brusquely. When a Black lady outside his truck knocked on his closed door, he added, "Give her a hand and no smart-ass remarks."

The Private climbed out. Seen up close, the lady was elderly.

"Those wooden benches in back are uncomfortable," he told her. "Ride up front. I'll sit back there."

"I'm tougher than I look," she said, starting around him, "and extremely well-padded as you can see."

Stepping in front of her, the Private said, "I want to do this, ma'am. Please let me."

"Thank you." The lady smiled. "That's very kind."

He helped her climb into the cab. Later she smiled at him through its rear window.

At her destination, she handed him cookies from her lunch.

In a single night, the Carl Young Riot had damaged more property than any predecessor. The destruction had no pattern. One block was left in ruins, and the next untouched. A twelve-block stretch of Century Boulevard—now called Charcoal Alley—had burned to the ground.

Those who'd gone through previous riots remembered trash piling up ... the despair of being without work because hundreds of businesses had been destroyed ... food shortages ... homeless people living in parks ... and no electricity, gas, or water.

Few, however, had foreseen that clothes at cleaners, cars left for mechanical work, and valuables pawned for a pittance would be destroyed and could never be reclaimed at any price.

Larry hadn't left his office for days. Too busy to go out for lunch, he'd had his assistant, Lois Brady, fill his office refrigerator with protein bars, apples, cottage cheese, yogurt, and celery. He ate as he worked, catnapped briefly when necessary, and too often treated himself to sugar-rich candy bars from a vending machine.

Napping when Lois Brady woke him, he rubbed his eyes.

"You said to wake you if Bob Pickering returned your call," she said, handing him a portable phone.

"Thanks for getting back to me, Bob," Larry greeted Governor Webster's aide. "A few weeks ago, two police officers arrested a man at the State Capitol Building for disorderly conduct. He wanted to tell Governor Webster about something he thought was going on in South Central.

"Yeah. Wade Hardin. He refused to leave without talking to the Governor personally. We couldn't get rid of him. He's a whacko."

"That's what I thought at first," Larry replied, "but now I'm not so sure. Do you have his address?"

"No, but LAPD should have it. I'll get it for you."

When Pickering called back, he told Larry, "The arresting officers took Harden home and checked on him a few days later. He'd moved without leaving a forwarding address."

—∾—

Next Larry looked in on Tony Jackson and Bill Pope. They were working on the Young People's Project. No longer required to wear his National Guard uniform, Tony was dressed in mulberry-colored slacks, a pale-lemon turtleneck pullover, and an olive-green double-breasted jacket.

In a room done completely in white—even the doorknobs—he stood out.

"How's it going?" Larry asked.

Bill Pope replied, "Beats hell out of driving people around."

"With the money you and Emily have raised so far," Tony said, "we can implement most of my programs."

"We won't stop," Larry assured him, "until we have enough for all of them. Emily's organizing a benefit concert at the Hollywood Bowl, and we've only solicited half of the businesses on our list."

"Tell the owners," Bill Pope suggested, "we're not giving kids something for nothing. They'll have to have excellent grades and get out of the gangs."

For days, Larry had slept fewer than his normal five hours. Both eyes, always dry, were worse than usual. He was in his office, instilling eye drops when Lois Brady buzzed him on the intercom.

"You have a call from General Nelson," she said.

"The mayor asked me to have my men camp outside the riot area," Nelson began. "He has no authority over me, but I'd like to maintain good relations with the civilian authorities. Could you kindly overrule him as if it's your idea? The Guard needs the locals' goodwill and cooperation, which we won't get if we're seen as outsiders who go home at night."

"I'll call him, praise what you're doing, and tell him I want it continued."

"Thank you, sir," Nelson said. "I appreciate your support."

"You and your men have more than earned it," Larry replied.

"After you raise the funds," Nelson told Larry respectfully, "I'll provide men and equipment to make that money go a lot further."

—~—

In 2001, the Los Angeles Unified School District bought and renovated a twenty-nine story headquarters in downtown L.A. They justified the cost by proposing to lease out the excess space, then expanded to fill it.

"That's the daytime home of about three thousand five hundred administrators," Tony muttered as he, Larry, and Don Maxwell walked from a nearby parking lot. "What an outrageous waste of money."

"Don't forget we're going there to ask a favor," Larry said, handing Tony a newspaper clipping. "Read this and see if you can find it in your heart to give 'em the benefit of the doubt."

They stopped while Tony read and Don Maxwell did what bodyguards do.

"Feel better now?" Larry asked when Tony looked up.

Having read the clipping in the car, Larry knew the statistics. L.A. Unified oversaw seven hundred schools, forty-six thousand teachers, seven hundred thousand students, and an annual budget of eight billion dollars.

It had its own police force, janitors, maintenance crews, and purchasing department. It also operated more buses than L.A.'s Metropolitan Transportation Authority, and served more meals than every McDonalds within 50 miles, combined.

Its directors had refused Larry's request to open twelve South Central schools during summer vacation. Those being the only facilities suitable for Tony's Young People's Project, Larry had requested a chance to change their minds.

At 9:00 AM, he and Tony were shown to side-by-side podiums facing the directors' table. The rest of the room was jammed with teachers, reporters, and television cameras.

L.A. School Superintendent Fernando Garcia thanked Larry and Tony for coming, then said, "As I already told you repeatedly, our budget is overstretched. We can't afford to keep those schools open or risk having them damaged."

"If you'll leave them open after regular school hours for the Young People's Project," Larry proposed, "they'll be staffed, operated, and protected by the National Guard. Its soldiers who are teachers will tutor students, and its counselors will advise them.

"At no cost to L.A. Unified, General Nelson will send carpenters, plumbers, electricians, concrete finishers, and roofers to rebuild portable classrooms damaged or destroyed by rioters. While doing that, they'll train teenage apprentices for whom local contractors are holding summer jobs."

After the teachers in the room gave Larry a standing ovation, the directors huddled.

Then Supervisor Garcia told Larry, "That's a deal we can live with. This afternoon we'll send a contract for General Nelson's signature."

—m—

On the way back to the car, Tony asked Larry, "Why did you make that offer?"

"Without those schools, the best of your programs will go down the drain. So I pulled it out of my hat when the Supervisor gave what he intended as his final no."

"You made a lot of promises. Can you keep them?"

"Sure. All we have to do is talk companies into donating building supplies, get General Nelson to send tradesmen, teachers, tutors, coaches, and the other people I promised, and then convince sporting goods companies to donate equipment and uniforms for athletic teams."

"That may be more difficult than you make it sound."

"The challenge will make it more enjoyable."

"All we can do is try," Tony said.

"No," Larry countered. "We can do our best."

"What's the difference?"

"When you try, you consider failure an option. When you do your best, you intend to succeed no matter what."

Emily's benefit concert was held at the Hollywood Bowl, twelve miles from the riot area. The morning of that event, Michael Bridges arrived at the hundred-year-old outdoor amphitheater to help with final preparations.

Already men had unloaded microphones, amplifiers, and other electronic equipment from trucks. On stage beneath its famous band shell, a man tuned a piano the old-fashioned way: push a key several times ... adjust the string with a tuning lever ... repeat until satisfied.

Opening the concert that night Emily thanked the Hollywood Bowl's directors for the use of their facility, the musicians for their time, and the audience for its generous support.

With all seventeen thousand seats occupied, Michael estimated they'd clear over five million dollars.

Later, sitting in the audience, he was enthralled by the solo of a Black woman, Regina Butler, in a tight high-necked red dress. Her back gracefully curved, she sat on the front edge of a chair and coaxed the overture from Mozart's *The Marriage of Figaro* from her expressive violin.

After that performance, Michael went backstage and introduced himself to Regina. As luck would have it, she lived in Sacramento, a half-mile from his house. He asked if she'd like to sit with him for the rest of the concert.

CHAPTER NINETEEN
COPS ON BIKES

THE AFTERNOON of the concert, Larry attended the funerals of two LAPD officers gunned down during the riot's first night. One was the son of an officer with whom he'd served.

When he got home, Emily was back from the Hollywood Bowl, listening to Gene Rice's program.

"For those who criticized LAPD officers for killing four rioters last week," Rice was saying, "I'd like to point out that the Civil War's New York Draft Riots were all-White insurrections suppressed by federal troops using Gatling guns and artillery. That's a far cry from the restraint shown during the Carl Young Riot."

Looking up, Emily told Larry, "You looked drained."

"I am," he said, putting a match to paper beneath logs and kindling she'd arranged in the fireplace.

"Have you had dinner?" she asked.

"I'm not hungry, thank you. How did LAPD become so hated by people in South Central?"

"We're both exhausted," she replied, "and I'm brain dead. Can we please do this in the morning?"

Reading in the library—long before Emily usually got up—Larry was startled when she came in wearing her bathrobe.

"It's hard," she began, "to imagine the enthusiasm of the first African-Americans who went to Los Angeles. By the early 1900s, eight thousand Black people lived there in multi-racial neighborhoods. A third of them owned their homes. W.E.B. Du Bois—a founder of the National Association for the Advancement of Colored People—called it 'a wonderful place.'"

She crossed her legs before continuing.

"Back then, LAPD was popular because they were keeping the Mafia out or at least controlling them. In extreme cases, undercover officers in plain clothes met mob bosses at the airport and took him up on Mulholland Drive. They killed a few. Others they beat beyond recognition and released as a message to the eastern Mafia.

"Prior to and during World War II, as many as ten thousand Negroes a month came to work in shipyards, aircraft production plants and on car assembly lines, making tanks. Dirt poor all their lives, they were suddenly earning enough to qualify for mortgages.

"Concerned about this influx, LAPD confined them to an area that didn't increase in size as its population grew. Whites elsewhere stopped selling or renting to them and used restrictive real estate covenants to keep them from moving into less congested areas.

"Their schools were inferior and didn't prepare them for jobs after the defense industry shut down. The situation worsened when automakers moved to Detroit and were replaced by new industries such as aerospace.

"White-owned stores sold them inferior merchandise—even rotting meat—at high prices. When they left their area,

LAPD and White youth gangs forced them back where they *belonged*. Police looked the other way when crosses were burned in their yards or they were shot at.

"A year before the Watts Riot, the National Urban League said Los Angeles offered Negroes a better life than any other American city. By then, Black unemployment was nine percent nationally and thirty-four percent in South Central.

"Harassed daily by police, Blacks focused their rage on LAPD. When their unnoticed misery exploded into the Watts Riot, officers made themselves all the more hated by fatally shooting more than thirty unarmed Blacks in the back.

"Characterizing the uprising as mindless violence, Chief William Parker publicly called the rioters 'monkeys in a zoo.'

"When reformers hired William Bratton as LAPD chief, he told subordinates, 'I am not accepting what you accept as a norm. This has got to stop.'

"But he was an outsider and couldn't change LAPD's us-against-the-world culture."

When she drew in a breath to continue, Larry raised his hand, stopping her.

"Enough," he said. "Listening to that was difficult. I can't imagine what it must have been like to live through it. I know from firsthand experience that if police patrolled White communities as they do Watts, it would provoke a revolution."

A flock of birds flew past the window, their shadows darting across the opposite wall.

—✻—

Los Angeles Police Department Chief Johnson's office was on the top floor of LAPD's headquarters. At the security checkpoint, Larry emptied his pockets and sent their contents and his briefcase through the X-ray machine, then walked through a metal detector and reclaimed his possessions.

At a bank of elevators, he took the next one and got off at the tenth floor. A secretary was waiting and led him to the Chief's office. She knocked on the door, then opened it.

The wall behind the chief's desk was covered with citations, awards, photographs, and a large laser carving of his badge. Across the room, an outdoor terrace faced City Hall, across the street.

Chief Johnson was LAPD's most reform-minded leader since William Bratton. He had droopy eyelids, sun-bleached flaxen hair, and razor-sharp creases in his blue serge trousers. Under him, LAPD had quadrupled its Black and Hispanic officers and excessive force complaints were declining.

On the edge of his desk was a plate of cold, half-eaten bacon, eggs, hash browns, and toast. Responsible for the behavior of over ten thousand officers, he looked exhausted.

"My condolences," Larry began, "on the officers who recently lost their lives. I'm deeply and sincerely sorry."

"The first day of this riot," Johnson grumped, rubbing his eyes, "was the bloodiest twenty-four hours in this department's history. Twenty-nine of my men were killed or wounded. And today the L.A. *Times* had the gall to run a story about a supposedly innocent bystander they shot.

"The article made it sound like they broke into the guy's living room and shot him while he was watching cartoons with his kids. If there were any innocent bystanders … "

Johnson's rant ended abruptly. He walked around his desk, gestured for Larry to sit in the chair across from him, and asked, "What can I do for you?"

"Nothing," Larry said. "I'm here to do something for you."

"Not offer me advice, I hope." Johnson managed a tight smile.

"No," Larry chuckled. "Chief Taylor in Sacramento tells me you tried to put some of your officers on bicycles and couldn't get funding."

"Damn shame. People don't trust cops sitting in air-conditioned cars with the windows closed. But the powers that be don't want cops on bicycles in a city too big to be adequately covered in squad cars."

"How many bicycles do you need?"

Johnson's interest sharpened.

"With thousands of soldiers in South Central and crime almost non-existent," he said, leaning forward, "this is the perfect time for a pilot program."

"How many bicycles?" Larry pressed.

"Even with a volume discount, they'll be expensive. We need some costly extras."

"I'm sold on the idea," Larry said. "What will it cost?"

"This is the lowest bid I got." Johnson took an invoice from a desk drawer and slid it toward Larry.

It was for nearly a half-million dollars.

"I doubt," Chief Johnson said, "the Governor's budget has that much of a surplus."

"That's for sure, but I have personal investments."

"You're serious?"

"I am."

"At the press conference where you announce this—"

"There won't be one," Larry interrupted. "Tell your superiors you received an anonymous donation and order the bicycles. I'll bring you a certified check this afternoon."

On his way to the elevator, Larry passed two senior LAPD officers who didn't see him coming.

"I wish White people who demonstrate for Black rights had been with me during the riot," one said. "They need to see the consequences of teaching civil disobedience to those animals."

—m—

When LAPD offered no-questions-asked amnesty to looters who returned stolen merchandise, comedians had what one of them called 'a late-night field day.'

Next morning when Larry came to work, Ted Roffman was in the conference room reading the *L.A. Times*.

"Morning," they greeted simultaneously.

"Any good news?" Larry asked.

"None better than this editorial." Ted folded his paper and read, "'All across South Central this morning, hundreds of appliances, computers, T.V. sets, etc. appeared as if by magic. Many still in the original boxes, they were found on curbs, outside police stations, in vacant lots, in front of stores from which they'd been stolen... you name it.'"

—m—

"You were right to let camera crews into the riot area over my objections," General Nelson told Larry as they sat facing each other in the general's office. "Their reports on the Guard's performance and restraint were overwhelmingly favorable."

He put a check mark beside the top item on his list and continued, "What do you want me to do with the rioters my men have taken into custody?"

"I thought," Larry said, "you were turning them over to LAPD."

"The jails are full. If they can't be arraigned within the required forty-eight hours, the American Civil Liberties Union will petition for their release."

"How many are serious offenders?"

"None. We turned those over to LAPD. The ones we're holding are facing fines at worst."

"We could divide them into teams big enough to paint a house in a few hours and turn 'em loose when they're finished."

"What houses?"

"How about those tagged with graffiti or otherwise defaced during the riot?"

"There's a law against using conscripted labor to benefit private individuals," Nelson said.

"In that case, we'll ask them to volunteer."

A smile tugged at the corners of Nelson's mouth.

"Sounds like I'm not the only frustrated social engineer in this conversation," he said. "Let's do it."

—∞—

"That's strange," Emily told Larry, looking out their bedroom window.

"What?" Larry asked.

"Earlier today, I saw the man in that car across from our driveway."

Larry aimed and focused the binoculars he'd bought for bird watching.

"Nothing to worry about," he said. "It's Darth Vader."

"Who?"

"Governor Webster's bodyguard."

Emily chuckled. "That can't be his real name."

"He legally changed it to Darth Vader. I have no idea what it was before that. I'll see why he's here."

In a full-length slicker, Larry walked down the glistening driveway through a light rain to Vader's car. As the driver's side window went down, he bent at the waist.

"My wife," he said, "thinks she saw you several times today."

"Not very observant, is she?" Vader grinned. "I've been following her for days."

"Why?" Larry asked as a brief downpour stopped drumming on Vader's car.

"Well," Vader drawled, "Don Maxwell is still providing security for Governor Webster. The man in charge of Protective Services is hunting in Alaska. His second in command is in South Central. Rather than get paid for nothing, I thought I'd watch over your wife."

"Why would anyone hurt her?"

"I'm not sure, but I suspect some crazy son of a bitch wants the Guard to go home and you're in his way."

Larry stared at his house, paused, and told Vader, "Go home and get some sleep. Tomorrow morning, I'll get you reassigned. Then you can protect both Emily and me."

Emily was in bed when Larry returned to their room. He glanced out the window. The car was gone.

"I'd like you to start working at my office," he told Emily. "You'll be safer there."

"I know you have a lot on your mind," she said, changing the subject, "but something came up unexpectedly. New Beginnings has two newborns available, a Black and a Japanese. They want to know if we'll take one, and I have to answer as soon as possible."

Larry had never considered adopting a Black baby, but he didn't consider that to be prejudice. After all, he'd admired Black Leaders' valiant struggle against racial injustice before being exposed to the criminals he'd met while policing his beat in South Central.

Furthermore, he could easily adopt a Japanese, something a racist would find difficult. He admired that hard-working race. Soon after coming to California as poor immigrants, they owned farms worth a hundred million 1941 dollars.

When their country of origin bombed Pearl Harbor, bringing America into World War II, Japanese-Americans produced nearly half of California's enormous vegetable crop. Following Pearl Harbor and President Roosevelt's declaration of war, the U.S.—worried about spies and saboteurs—confiscated their properties and locked them up in camps until Japan surrendered, four years later.

After leaving the internment camps, the Japanese-Americans started with nothing for the second time, and most bounced back to become prosperous again. How could anyone not admire them?

"Let's go see those babies," Larry said, joining Emily at breakfast the following morning.

"Someone adopted the Japanese baby," she told him. "We'll have to take the other or stay on the waiting list."

When he hesitated, she said, "You're right. This is the wrong time to take on the responsibility of raising a child. We should wait until I'm no longer working."

Sadly, Emily had taken Larry's long pause to mean he was reluctant to adopt a Black child. But he'd been considering how it might affect that child to have parents with demanding jobs. They'd been on the same page, but it would seem self-serving if he said that.

CHAPTER TWENTY
THE TIME-HONORED FORMULA OF COWARDS

"THERE'S NO point in continuing to discuss the prevention of something that's already happened," Larry began Tuesday's meeting of the Race Relations Commission. "It's time to thank you for your hard work and ask if any of you are available to help with the Young People's Project."

Predictably, Dolores Menke, Ron Jardine and Horace Grayson raised their hands. The Commission's members had heard testimony from psychologists, historians, sociologists, business executives, and a talk show host. Yet none had noticeably changed his or her opinions on race.

A woman, whose name Larry couldn't recall, raised her hand. She hadn't spoken at previous meetings.

"I'm a teacher and president of our union," she began. "I'm sure that's why Governor Webster appointed me to this Commission. I'm disappointed by our failure to address discrimination against Hispanics.

"During the Rodney King riot, Hispanics were a third of those killed and half of those arrested. My brother—God rest his soul—was one of them. I don't want to simply help. I want to make a difference. I'll gladly give up my summer vacation to teach at South Central's summer schools."

"I'm sorry," Larry said, "but I've forgotten your name."

"Angela Rodriguez."

"Angela, if you're free this afternoon, I'll introduce you to Tony Jackson so you can get started."

—∞—

Larry had set aside the coming weekend to show potential donors the benefits of the Young People's Project, with help from the media. Bright and early Saturday morning, Darth Vader drove him, Emily, and Tony to an oceanfront dock in La Jolla, near San Diego.

There, students waited to board a Scripps Institute oceanographic research vessel.

"No one," a nearby White reporter told another, "ever gave me a free two-day ocean voyage."

"No one gave these students one either," Larry clarified. "This isn't charity. It's an investment in America's future. These youngsters are the top summer school students in the South Central Young People's Project, and they earned this."

After the relatively short drive to La Cañada, Larry, Emily, Tony and newsman Brian Waterman joined science students at the Jet Propulsion Laboratory. There they sat in on a presentation by Bob Mitchell, who'd been in charge of the Cassini-Huygens robotic spacecraft when it collected data on Saturn and its moons.

They listened as long as they dared and reluctantly left.

Back in their car Larry said, "The kids don't seem to be enjoying this as much as I expected."

"They've learned to keep their feelings inside," Tony said. "Believe me, they're having the time of their lives."

Looking out the window as they left the Laboratory grounds, Larry saw demonstrators carrying signs and chanting: "Get the Guard Gone!"

—~—

At the Mount Palomar Observatory, Larry's group was greeted by Brian Waterman and a photographer.

Once inside, Tony said, "This is the first time some of these kids have ever been outside of South Central. Can you imagine how they must feel?"

Twenty Black students were waiting their turns at the big telescope.

"That's Saturn," a Black man was explaining. "Its rings are made up of trillions of ice particles that rotate around it."

"Why does that instructor look familiar?" Larry asked quietly.

"His picture," Emily whispered, "has been in the newspapers all week. He's Gibor Basri, a professor of astronomy at the University of California."

Back outside, Larry took questions from Waterman while the cameraman shot video, protecting Darth Vader's identity by making certain he wasn't in it.

"According to a reputable source," Waterman said, "President Ripley may federalize California's National Guard and withdraw it."

"Ripley can believe it or not," Larry quipped, "but the Guard has done no end of good."

A fitting end to Larry's perfect day started as he came out of a nearby hotel's bathroom in pajamas. Sitting on a couch, Emily repeatedly crooked her finger, beckoning.

"Lie on your back with your head in my lap," she said.

Once upon a time, that invitation had inevitably led to long, slow, lovemaking.

"Too bad you spent so much time in the shower," Emily said, running her fingers through his hair. "You missed the late-night news."

"Did our tour get any publicity?"

"CNN, ABC, NBC, and CBS all featured Brian Waterman's report, including your 'Ripley can believe it or not' quote."

Slowly, one-by-one, she undid the buttons on his pajama top, then untied the bottoms.

"Tonight," she told him, "you'll be warm enough without these."

CHAPTER TWENTY-ONE
NO JUSTICE, NO PEACE

SUNDAY'S SCHEDULE was less hectic. Larry and Emily slept in, then joined Tony and Darth Vader for breakfast. At mid-morning, Vader drove them to the old mission in San Juan Capistrano.

Founded in the 1700s on *El Camino Real,* The Royal Road, it had been operated by priests and monks whose duties included Christianizing local Indians and providing a rest stop for travelers. Rebuilt or refurbished after several earthquakes, it had become a tourist attraction annually visited by hundreds of thousands.

Emily and Larry tagged along during the Y.P.P.'s guided tour.

"The kids," Emily whispered, "are enjoying this much more than I thought they would."

"This was once thought to be the oldest standing building in America," the guide told them in the Serra Chapel.

"Whoever thought that," one of the girls said, "never saw my house."

"So much for keeping their feelings inside," Larry teased Tony.

"I'm at least as surprised as you," Tony said, shaking his head.

When the tour ended, the Mission's executive director came out of his office to address the Y.P.P. students.

"San Juan Capistrano," he began, "is a leading attraction in a state that's full of them. We're proud that a hundred thousand students a year come here to learn about California's past. Please come back soon with your friends and families."

Larry, Emily, and Darth Vader thanked the Executive Director for his hospitality, then boarded a National Guard helicopter for Edward's Air Force Base. There, more Y.P.P. honor students were waiting for the latest space shuttle to land.

—~—

Of eight thousand people arrested during the Carl Young Riot, two thousand lesser offenders had been released due to overcrowded jails. To expeditiously bring the others to trial, hundreds of pending legal matters had been postponed, and dockets had been cleared in most of the county's six hundred courtrooms.

On the first day of trials, Avery King led a demonstration at the Clara Shortridge Foltz Criminal Justice Center in downtown L.A. The protesters—disorganized at first—broke into spontaneous chants which slowly unified into the ominous 'No Justice, No Peace' of the Watts Riot.

When all the courtrooms were full, LAPD officers shut the building's entry doors. In the plaza outside, family members of those to be tried that day were interviewed. Then the media left to cover other stories.

Switching on his bullhorn, Avery King implored the crowd, "Tomorrow, same time, same place. Bring your friends and families."

—~—

Muhammad Nasheed's top lieutenants were also in the courthouse plaza that morning. Rather than risk being seen by his father, Nasheed himself was elsewhere. His father, Avery

King, was doing a masterful job of manipulating South Central's angry, alienated residents.

—~—

The request for National Guard troops to keep order at L.A. County's courts originated with District Attorney Benedict Welch. First it went to the Mayor who forwarded it to General Nelson. He had it couriered to the Governor's office, and Ted Roffman took it to Larry.

"Shall I get General Nelson on the phone?" Ted asked.

"Yes," Larry replied. Then, on his intercom, he invited Michael Bridges and Emily to join them.

When Larry finished explaining the situation, Bridges softly said, "It's wrong to keep people from peacefully exercising their civil rights... not to mention that using guardsmen for that purpose will make South Central regret having welcomed them."

Pointing at Ted, Larry asked, "Your thoughts?"

"We can't have mobs intimidating jurors, period," Roffman snapped.

"There's another option," Emily offered. "We could meet the demonstrators' demands. Here's what I have in mind."

—~—

Skipping dinner that night, Larry and his advisers spent hours on phones. This time, people who'd turned a deaf ear to South Central's 'No, Justice, No Peace' chant for decades listened with their hearts.

By midnight, Courtroom Live Network was preparing to show the trials free on public television. Preparations were also underway to accommodate the expected crowds at twelve courthouses.

Shriners had delivered folding chairs and tables, sunshades, and outdoor grills, bearing the 'Love to the Rescue' logo of the Shriner's non-profit children's hospitals. Owners of grocery stores had donated food, and Shriners were standing by to cook it.

At the downtown courthouse plaza, loudspeakers were playing a recording. Hearing its message, protesters with loved ones scheduled for trial that day rushed home to watch Courtroom Live or stayed to see the trials on large screens in the plaza while enjoying free omelets, sizzling bacon, and toast.

CHAPTER TWENTY-TWO
BLACK SEPARATISTS

FOR WEEKS, the trials produced newsworthy oddities. A girl's boyfriend was convicted of murdering her and trying to make it look as if she'd died in a fire during the riot.

—~—

An adult and his teen-age son—arrested at the same time by the same officer as they came out of the same store with identical television sets—were tried separately. In regular court, charges against the adult were dropped. In juvenile court, the teenager was convicted.

—~—

Of particular interest to Larry Winslow, a man was acquitted of murdering Wade Hardin—who'd tried to warn Governor Webster that someone was uniting South Central's gangs. According to the District Attorney, the accused had shot Hardin before the riot and later put the corpse in a burned-out building. He was acquitted.

—~—

For centuries, America's Blacks had fought for integration and equality. But whenever those goals seemed within reach,

Whitey had made them vanish like mirages, only to reappear farther away.

Muhammad Nasheed's ultimate goal had been inspired by Black separatists such as Martin Delany. Born free, he'd been a Major during America's Civil War and was later dismissed from Harvard Medical School after White students protested his presence.

Convinced Blacks had no future in the U.S., Delaney had advocated the establishment of Black nations in the West Indies, South America or Africa.

—ɷ—

The Right Excellent Marcus Garvey, a Jamaican Black nationalist and founder of the United Negro Improvement Association, had dreamt of unifying Africa and serving as its first president.

—ɷ—

Benjamin 'Pap' Singleton had established modestly successful Black colonies in Kansas, the largest of which soon had to be financially supported by the Presbyterian Church.

More recently, America's Nation of Islam had also called for an independent Black utopia on American soil.

—ɷ—

Because they were started from scratch, these would-be paradises had all failed. Muhammad Nasheed's would be different. South Central already had infrastructure, an economy, taxes, a government, and schools. With him in charge it would be independent—much like America's Indian Reservations.

Whitey would accept this fait accompli or pay a terrible price. Nasheed was allied with America's most implacable foes. Assisted by Iran's fundamentalists, he'd establish a totalitarian government and Sharia Law.

True believers would support him with the fervor demanded by their holy book, the Koran, which warned its followers: 'Turn not your backs on believers marching to war. Whosoever does this becomes deserving of Allah's wrath and his abode shall be Hell; an evil destination.'

CHAPTER TWENTY-THREE
A RUSSIAN BULLET

AFTER DAYS of deliberations, the judge presiding over Walter Jezierski's trial declared a hung jury. Shortly after Jezierski was released, Larry Winslow called General Nelson.

"All's quiet," Nelson told him, "except for some minor protests and looting. It helps that the FBI is making significant progress in the Carl Young investigation. They found a bullet where he was shot and are checking it for DNA. It's from a Russian 7N31 armor-piercing cartridge.

"They also had Tony Jackson listen when they interrogated a suspicious curfew violator. He was careful about what he said, but Tony detected slogans taught in Iran's Muslim *madrasas,* where disaffected Middle Eastern males are taught to hate America and everything we represent.

"Tony has befriended him and plans to take him along when he goes hiking on Mt. Whitney this weekend."

A hundred thirty-five miles north of Los Angeles in Central California's Sierra Nevada Mountains, Mount Whitney is the highest point in the lower forty-eight states. First successfully climbed in 1873, its rugged slopes are eighty-five miles from North America's lowest point, Badwater Basin in Death Valley.

Saturday morning at dawn, Tony Jackson parked his souped-up Ford Mustang at Whitney Portal, where the Mt. Whitney trail begins.

His companion, who insisted his name was simply Kamasi, had been quiet during the drive.

"We're now more or less eight thousand feet above sea level," Tony said as they stood on opposite sides of his car, stretching, "and roughly that far below the summit. It's a twenty-two mile round trip and takes most people two days. Wanna try to make it in one?"

"I was on my school's cross-country track team," Kamasi replied.

"That was then and this is now," Tony said, opening his Mustang's trunk. "You sure you're in good enough shape to try this?"

"There's one way to find out," Kamasi said.

"You'll need this." Tony handed him a backpack.

"What's in here?"

"A canteen, granola bars, trail mix, apples, and yogurt-covered raisins. That'll keep you going until we get back. Good thing we ate in the car. We'll make better time before the trail's crowded. You go first. I'll try to keep up."

Quietly they passed through a campground where people were sleeping in pup tents. After that, the trail darkened and narrowed.

"There's a flashlight," Tony said, "in the side pocket of your pack."

Kamasi switched it on and searched the surrounding area.

"Any bears or mountain lions up here?" he asked.

"Quite a few. Don't worry. If a mountain lion attacks, you won't see it coming."

First light revealed the emerald-green meadow at Outpost Camp. There a group of hikers who'd spent the night started up the trail ahead, looking back over their shoulders.

"They look sorry to see brothers out here," Kamasi said.

"More likely they're surprised," Tony said. "Blacks are an unusual sight out here. This is the third time I've hiked Mt. Whitney, and the only brothers I've seen were the ones I brought."

At green, glacial Mirror Lake, they refilled their canteens. Next, a series of switchbacks took them above the treeline. From there, they saw the rising sun change surrounding peaks from white to pink to fiery orange. By then, Kamasi had fallen behind.

"That side of the mountain," Tony said, pointing west, "goes all the way down to Sequoia National Park, as beautiful a place as I've ever seen. I'll take you there sometime if you want."

Above ten thousand feet, the trail narrowed, making drop offs more threatening. In the oxygen-poor air, Kamasi sat down on a granite boulder.

"Got a headache and feel dizzy?" a man going the other way asked.

Kamasi nodded.

"That's because you're having difficulty adjusting to the altitude." The man handed Kamasi a container of yogurt and a bottle of Gatorade. "Eat the yogurt, wait a bit, then drink the Gatorade. Don't turn around this close to your goal. Slow down. And you'll make it. Good luck."

"People are friendlier out here than in cities," Tony said. "Take a breather, then we'll go the rest of the way. You'll never forgive yourself if you miss the view from the top."

After reaching the summit and returning to where they'd started that morning, they took a nap in Tony's car, then headed for South Central.

"I ache in places I didn't know I have," Kamasi said as the miles flashed past. "But getting all the way to the top and back down in one day was worth the pain."

Elated by his accomplishment, Kamasi was talkative throughout the drive.

"Where do you go to school?" Tony asked when an opportunity came.

"I don't go to a regular school," Kamasi answered.

"Don't tell me. Let me guess. A Catholic school."

"No, a Muslim school, a *madrasa*."

Rather than lose Kamasi's hard-won trust, Tony changed the subject. When they went to Sequoia National Park in a week, he'd try to find out where that *madrasa* was.

CHAPTER TWENTY-FOUR
PISTOLS FOR TWO AND COFFEE FOR ONE

DAYS BEFORE Larry's State of the State address to California's Legislature, he was at his computer, still working on it. He'd rejected his speechwriter's first four drafts and was trying to salvage the fifth when Lois Brady handed him an envelope with an unfamiliar return address.

The handwritten note inside read:

'I admire what you're doing in South Central. If I can help with your State of the State speech, all you have to do is ask.

'I assume its main purpose will be to get more funding for South Central?

'Regards,

'Hallie Martin.'

Larry sent for Michael Bridges.

"I just received this," he told Bridges, handing over Hallie's note.

"Hallie Martin." Bridges raised his eyebrows. "She's among the best speechwriters in America. Rumor has it she wrote the best two paragraphs of President Lyndon Johnson's speech urging passage of the 1965 Voting Rights Bill. I'll be right back."

He returned and placed a photocopy on Larry's desk.

Looking down, Larry silently read: 'Our lives have been marked with debate about great issues, issues of war and peace, issues of prosperity and depression.

'But seldom does an issue lay bare the secret soul of America itself. Rarely are we met by a challenge, not to our growth or abundance, or our welfare or our security, but rather to the values and the purposes and meaning of our beloved nation.

'The issue of equal rights for American Negroes is such an issue. And should we defeat every enemy, and should we double our wealth and conquer the stars and still be unequal to this issue, we will have failed as a people and as a nation.'

"Wow!" Larry exclaimed. "That's impressive."

—m—

As usual before their Monday morning meeting, Larry, Emily, Ted and Michael were in the lunch room enjoying fresh donuts and coffee.

"Congratulations are in order," Ted said. "Michael got engaged Saturday."

"Who's the lucky lady?" Emily asked.

"Regina Bradley," Michael replied, "the violin player I met at your Hollywood Bowl benefit concert."

"Congratulations," Larry said.

"Don't marry her until the two of you no longer feel romantic toward each other," Roffman advised gruffly. "You won't really know her before that."

"Careful," Larry teased Michael. "Taking marital advice from a three-times-divorced curmudgeon is like asking Colonel Sanders to watch over your chickens."

The room's paging system speaker crackled.

"Governor Winslow, Chief Johnson at LAPD is on line two."

"I want to thank you," the Chief began, "for helping me get some of my men out of squad cars and on bicycles. "It's gone even better than I expected. Officers' attitudes have improved now that they're meeting the people they protect. And residents are calling to say how much they like the new officers, even though they're the same ones who were in the squad cars."

"By my count," Larry said, "that's *two* big steps."

Larry paused when Lois Brady knocked on his door, something she never did when he was on the phone.

"Sorry to interrupt," she apologized. "You have a call from President Ripley on line five."

"I'll get back to you," Larry told Chief Johnson and pressed the line five button.

"Please hold for the President of the United States," he heard.

Emily, Ted, and Michael left the room.

Larry was beginning to suspect this was one of Ted Roffman's practical jokes when he detected a Boston accent he'd heard countless times on television.

"Governor Winslow, I hope you're well."

"I am, thank you Mr. President. It's an honor to receive your call."

"How's that beautiful California weather? We're in the middle of a cold spell here."

"This is the best time of year in Sacramento," Larry replied. "Not too hot and not too cold."

"You have the National Guard in Los Angeles long after the riot area was stabilized. May I ask why?"

"Of course, but I'd rather show you. Why don't you have Air Force One make an extra stop when you come to San Francisco next week?"

"I'm up for re-election in November and have a full schedule. But I'll see if my Chief of Staff can shoehorn that in. He'll keep you informed."

After Larry hung up, Ted came in without knocking.

"What did the President want?" he asked.

"To know why the Guard is still in South Central," Larry replied.

"Was he pushy about it?"

"Not in the least. In fact, he was quite polite and deferential."

"He can afford to be low-key," Ted groused. "He has the whip hand. He can federalize the Guard and order them out. If dueling hadn't gone out of style, you could order pistols for two and coffee for one. That will be the only way to stop him if he gets the impression you're a racist."

—∾—

Once inside the California State Legislature's chambers, Larry walked the green carpeted aisle to a podium on an E-shaped platform. He drew only subdued applause from waiting Senate and Assembly members.

His audience was overwhelmingly opposed to more funding for South Central. Hallie Martin's masterpiece didn't plead with them to change their minds. It tried to get them to listen with their hearts.

For days Larry had rehearsed. Now he tried to do Hallie's speech justice. Unusual, it began with Reconstruction after the Civil War when former slaves were given citizenship, elected to local, state, and federal offices, and then helped draft new constitutions for slave states.

Then her words described the alarm when officials sent to administer the Reconstruction Acts after the Civil War proved more interested in lining their pockets than in noble goals.

Hallie's words mourned Reconstruction's collapse, after Federal troops withdrew and the South replaced the

Reconstruction Acts with Jim Crow laws, the Ku Klux Klan flourished, and landowners reduced Black sharecroppers to the equivalent of slaves.

"We hear much," Larry read from a teleprompter, "of the lynchings and intimidation that followed, but little about the countless petty humiliations.

"White merchants refused to use the then-courteous Miss, Mrs. or Mr. when billing Negros. By law, Blacks couldn't play checkers with Whites. Students in White schools refused to touch textbooks that had been used in Black schools. Public employees were fired for joining the NAACP.

"A Black dancer at the only Las Vegas casino with facilities for Black patrons went swimming in its pool and was asked to leave, after which the pool was drained, scrubbed, and refilled with 'clean' water."

Larry paused, then continued.

"One million two hundred thousand Negro soldiers, helped the U.S. win World War II. A Black colonel, Rupert Stanley Trimmingham, wrote two letters to *Yank*, the Army's Weekly Magazine, calling attention to the difficult position of America's Black soldiers in that conflict. These are excerpts from the first:

"'What is the Negro soldier fighting for? On whose team are we playing? Myself and eight other soldiers were on our way from Camp Claiborne, Louisiana, to the hospital here at Fort Huachuca. We had to lay over until the next morning for our train.

"'The next day we couldn't purchase a cup of coffee at any of the lunchrooms. The only place that would serve us was the railroad station, but of course we had to stay in the kitchen.

"'While eating, we saw German prisoners of war with American guards, enter the lunchroom, sit at the tables, enjoy their meals, talk, and smoke.

"'Looking on, I couldn't help but ask myself: are these men sworn enemies of my country? Are they not taught to hate and destroy all democratic governments? Are we not American soldiers, sworn to fight against them and die if need be?

"'Then why are they treated better? Why are we pushed around like cattle? If we are fighting for and dying for our country, why does the Government allow us to be treated as we are?

"'Some of the boys are saying you will not print this letter. I'm betting you will.'

"In a follow-up letter, Trimmingham thanked the editor of *Yank* for publishing his first letter and reported that he'd received 287 responses, 83 from sympathetic Whites. He went on to say: 'A strange feature about these letters is that most were from the Deep South.

"'Their writers are all proud to be of the South but are ashamed to learn that so many of their own people—by their actions and manner toward the Negro—are playing Hitler's game. It also pains me to know there are thousands of Whites willing to fight for this Frankenstein and keep him alive.

"'All the Negro is asking for is to be given half a chance to demonstrate that he is loyal and would give his life for this wonderful country if necessary.'

"Tragically," Larry continued, no longer reading, "Black soldiers disembarking from ships that brought them home after that war were greeted by signs sending Whites one way and them to rejoin the underclass.

"America can and should celebrate the progress she has made, but without forgetting there's much still to be done. African-Americans' ancestors built America's economy in the cotton, tobacco, indigo and sugar fields. They started this country down the road to greatness without pay or thanks. The least we can do is to help their descendants help themselves. But instead we've persecuted them—not only during slavery—and in ways that are painful for me to acknowledge.

"A notable example was Mississippi's Governor, James Vardaman, one of America's most notable racist politicians. During his 1903 campaign, he said, a vote for him was "a vote for White supremacy" and for quelling "the arrogant spirit" aroused in Blacks by [President Theodore] Roosevelt and his henchmen. Later he pledged that, "If necessary, every Negro in the state will be lynched."

He and other prominent elected officials encouraged the lynching of countless Black men accused by White women of looking at, talking to, assaulting, and/or or raping them.

The Tulsa Race Massacre—during which as many as 300 Black people were murdered—was reportedly ignited by a Black man who unintentionally stepped on the toe of a White female elevator operator.

Larry was uncharacteristically quiet as Darth Vader drove him and Emily home that night.

"It doesn't seem possible," he broke his silence, "that Hallie's speech received such a tepid response."

"It was brilliantly written and delivered," Emily told him gently. "Speeches like that don't arouse emotions. They make people think. It's too early to judge this one a failure. Remember the words in Dire Strait's song *Why Worry?*"

She cleared her throat and quietly sang:

'There should be laughter after pain
'There should be sunshine after rain
'These things have always been the same
'Why worry now?'

After getting out of the car, Emily took Larry's hand, led him to the dinner table she'd set for two, and dropped a napkin in his lap. After serving his favorite meal—corned beef and cabbage a la Emily—from her slow cooker, she turned off the lights and struck a foot-long match.

The shadow between her breasts deepened as she leaned forward and lit two twelve-inch red candles between them. Larry couldn't remember her ever displaying herself like that.

Better yet, she'd clearly done it on purpose.

CHAPTER TWENTY-FIVE
THE KILLING FIELD

SATURDAY MORNING, guardsmen in t-shirts and shorts disembarked from trucks in Ted Watkins Memorial Park. With bags of equipment slung across their shoulders, they started for the facilities hosting that day's Y.P.P. baseball, basketball, tennis, and football tournaments.

On his way to the basketball courts, Tony saw a poster prominently displayed on a nearby tree.

"How long has that been there?" he asked his opposing coach.

"I didn't see it yesterday."

Tony tore it down, rolled it up and put it under one arm like a swagger stick.

"What does it say?" a female volunteer asked. "All I could make out was 'Nazi.'"

"Apparently," Tony said grimly, "they're holding a rally here on Friday. They wouldn't have the nerve if the Guard wasn't here to protect them."

"We could pull out for a few days," she said, only half in jest.

"There's more than one way to skin a cat," Tony told her. "I've got a better idea."

By the time General Nelson arrived for the tournament's opening ceremony, guardsmen had taken the posters down.

"These were all over the park, Sir," Tony said, handing one over. "The Nazi Party thinks they're having a rally here."

"They are." Nelson sighed. "They have a permit, all nice and legal. We hung a lot of red tape in the way, hoping they'd give up, but even Nazis have constitutional rights."

"Well, if they can't be stopped, I can damn sure arrange for them to regret putting themselves in a vulnerable position."

"What do you have in mind?" Nelson asked.

"Arranging for their free publicity to show them in the bad light they deserve."

"First, clear whatever you're going to do with me."

The morning of the Nazi rally, guardsmen fanned out across Ted Watkins Park. Before nearby residents were out of bed, they had enclosed a soccer-field-size area with portable security barriers and erected a stage at one end. Tony nicknamed this enclosure The Killing Field.

Big news for days, the Nazi rally attracted reporters from every major network. Of the three cameramen with Brian Waterman, KTLA's News Director, two filmed guardsmen making a precautionary sweep of the park with metal detectors and bomb-sniffing dogs. The other filmed Waterman's interviews with spectators waiting at openings through the park's exterior chain link fence.

At the scheduled time, the Guard opened the access to walk-through metal detectors. After passing through them, spectators sat around The Killing Field's perimeter on blankets, sheets of plastic and cardboard, looking up at KTLA's helicopter.

Later, vans brought uniformed Nazis. After frisking them, the Guard escorted their group to the newly erected stage. Some climbed its stairs and sat on folding chairs. The others stood, backs to the stage, hands clasped behind their backs.

"You must hate those bastards," Brian Waterman said to Tony.

"I don't understand them," Tony responded, "but I've learned that hating someone only lets that person effortlessly hurt me."

"Would you repeat that on camera?" Waterman asked.

"Maybe later." Tony rushed toward arriving school buses with a bullhorn.

"He's up to something," Waterman told his cameraman. "Stick with him and film it."

Students got off the buses, then marched through the security barrier's gate. Inside, they formed five by five blocks of twenty-five each until The Killing Field was covered with these formations.

Thin and restless, the American Nazi Party's spokesman walked to the microphone and adjusted its height. Decades earlier, he'd have given a much different speech from the one on the pages he'd put on the lectern.

After undergoing several name changes—including one to the National Socialist White People's Party—his organization had gone back to being the American Nazi Party. Interested in establishing themselves as a legitimate political force, its leaders no longer referred to Adolf Hitler or displayed the swastika. They had also changed their rallying cry from "Sieg Heil" to "White Power."

"America needs the structure and stability destroyed by the Civil Rights Movement," the Nazi spokesman began nervously. "Granting unlimited rights to some groups has resulted in our great nation's cities being destroyed by riots, its schools being dragged down by undisciplined, unmotivated students, and its police overwhelmed by violent crime."

"We must impose order on people who won't impose it on themselves. We can no longer permit them to behave here as they would in the countries from which their ancestors came. We—"

The microphone went dead. Tony waved to men working on the park's electrical transformer.

"Sorry," he said through his bullhorn. "We've been having electrical problems. Fixing them won't take long." He pointed to a square of students and told the Nazi spokesman, "These boys are on Martin Luther King High School's track team." He paused, then asked "Who's your best sprinter?" Another pause. "Middle distance runner?' A third pause. Marathoner?"

"No one's denying that Blacks have certain physical abilities," the spokesman replied, his no-longer-amplified voice now faint.

"Of course Black people are fast on their feet," a skinhead outside the security barrier shouted. "After centuries of running from lions, the slow ones have all been eaten."

Ignoring him, Tony turned back toward the stage.

"Pick your five best basketball players," he said. "We'll step over to one of the courts and have a game."

"That won't prove anything." The skinhead again. "We can't be expected to run and jump like people who lost their tails only a few generations ago."

Raising his hand for silence, Tony continued, "Perhaps you think White superiority is intellectual more than physical? If so, meet Willis Washington." He pointed to a scrawny boy in another square. "He's not much for sports, but pretty good at math. I'll give this hundred dollar bill to any of you who can outscore him on a standard calculus test." He held it up.

"One exception to the rule doesn't prove much, does it?" Tony continued. "Okay, I'll give this to anyone in your group who outscores even one of Willis' classmates."

Quitting while he was ahead, Tony said, "Time for these youngsters to get back to school. They still have a lot to learn."

He waved his hand above his head. The students marched in formation from The Killing Field as they'd rehearsed. Parents who'd hesitated to sign permission slips for this particular field trip cheered.

Passing Tony, Willis Washington—struggling to conceal a grin—said, "We showed those Whites."

"We showed those *Nazis*," Tony corrected.

As the Nazis silently watched their audience leave, Brian Waterman told his closest cameraman, "Film this."

Microphone in hand, he stood in the foreground and summarized the day: "After the Black Muslims' 1995 Million Man March on Washington, D.C., the American Nazi Party circulated an email that went spectacularly viral. It mocked the March's message of personal responsibility with photographs of park crews cleaning up tons of trash demonstrators had left on the National Mall. There won't be a similar Nazi email after today's rally. As you see behind me, these spectators are picking up their own litter."

CHAPTER TWENTY-SIX
SENDING THEM BACK TO AFRICA

"TODAY'S SHOW," Gene Rice told his radio audience, "is the first of ten to be broadcast from Martin Luther King High School's auditorium. During the next two weeks, honor students and I will discuss and sometimes debate the future of America's increasingly multi-racial society.

"They are free to disagree with me but must support their opinions with facts, figures, and references.

"Last weekend, Taye Sanford and I visited Baldwin Park in the San Gabriel Valley region of Los Angeles County. It has a mostly non-White population of approximately a hundred thousand, and most people there earn good money and live comfortable lives.

"Would you like to live there, Taye?"

"Sure, especially in one of those big houses."

"Do any African-Americans or Hispanics live in those mansions?"

"Yeah. Lots."

"How do you know?"

"We went up and knocked on a door. A brother answered. You told him who you are and asked if he owned that house. He said yes and that he doesn't like your show and almost never agrees with you."

The other students burst into laughter.

"You could've left out that last part," Rice said.

"No. You made me promise to tell the whole truth."

"That I did." Rice chuckled. "What happened next?"

"We picked out another house and you knocked on that door. A real nice Black man answered. He showed us around the neighborhood in his Mercedes. I got to sit in front, and you had to sit in back."

The students had a second laugh at Rice's expense.

"Since you're telling the whole truth," Rice said, "let everyone know what that man said about me."

"He said you're right when you tell people Blacks can be successful if they take your advice."

"And do what?"

"You know," Taye paused, then imitated Rice's distinctive voice as he continued, "Stay in school, get good grades, don't get in trouble with the law, keep away from alcohol and drugs, work hard, and—"

"Don't have children," another student interrupted, "until you're financially and emotionally ready."

"I do harp on that," Rice acknowledged. "That's because it's the best advice a young person can get."

"But you say it too fucking often," Taye said.

"Taye, do you see that man over there?" Rice asked, pointing.

"Yeah."

"It's his job to bleep out swear words so my listeners won't be offended. If you want people to hear everything you say, please don't use profanity."

"Okay. Sorry."

"Now," Rice continued, "Your homework for tomorrow. In the early 1800s, before the Civil War, there were over

200,000 free Blacks in the United States. They were ex-slaves who'd purchased their freedom, had it bought for them by abolitionists, or been freed by provisions in their masters' wills. Many were having difficulty fitting into American society.

"Believing they'd have better lives elsewhere, the American Colonization Society bought land in northwest Africa with government and private funds. There it founded a new country and named it Liberia—after the Latin word for freedom. Then they offered to resettle free Blacks there."

"They just sent Black people away?" one of the girls asked.

"No one was forced to go," Rice said. "During the next half century, about fifteen thousand freedmen went to Liberia, but more than two hundred thousand stayed in the U.S., the only home they'd ever known.

"Read up on Liberia tonight. Tomorrow we'll discuss what life was like for those who went back to Africa."

—∞—

"Time to find out who did his or her homework," Gene Rice began his next broadcast. "What's the capital and largest city in Liberia?"

"Monrovia," one of the girls answered.

"Very good, Lanelle," Rice said. "Why was that name chosen?"

"It was named after James Monroe because he was president when Liberia was founded."

"Right. Who were the Americo-Liberians?"

"The people who went to Liberia from America," another girl, Amira Barkley, replied.

"Tell me about the first of these settlers."

Consulting her notes, Amira said, "They went on an American Colonization Society ship, the *Elizabeth,* and were escorted by a U.S. Navy warship."

"What did they do when they got to Liberia?"

"At first they struggled just to survive in their hostile, unfamiliar surroundings. Then they set out to build a new republic, based on the only culture and institutions they knew.

"They made English the official language. Their constitution and flag were based on America's. Their government had the same three branches—executive, legislative and judicial—which functioned like those in the U.S. The official currency was the Liberian dollar, and U.S. currency was also legal tender. In short, they created a democracy much like the one they'd left."

Rice paused, then asked, "How were these immigrants received by the people already there?"

Silence.

"The indigenous population," Rice said, "consisted of sixteen ethnic groups, mostly local tribes. Some fought for what they considered their land, but in vain because the Americos had U.S. backing and weapons.

"A mere five percent of the population, the more-educated Americos, ruled the country for over a century before a violent revolt removed them from power.

"During that time, unfortunately, they treated the natives the way their American masters had treated them. They denied indigenous peoples the right to vote and withheld jobs from non-Christians. Some even worked their plantations with slaves."

"It must have felt totally weird," Taye interrupted, "to have that much power after being discriminated against all their lives."

"Why do you think the Americos misused their power," Rice asked, frowning, "to oppress Liberia's other peoples? They knew how that feels."

Silence.

"Does anyone besides me get the impression that living up to ideals is difficult no matter who or where you are? How many of you would leave the United States to live in Liberia?"

Taye Sanford raised his hand.

"Are you sure, Taye? Life expectancy there is less than fifty years versus eighty-three in the U.S. It's one of the world's poorest countries. Salaries are a tiny fraction of what you'll earn here if you finish school.

"Illiteracy is twice as high. Five times as many people are below the poverty line. A third are malnourished. Only a quarter have access to clean water. Be sure to get a round-trip ticket."

CHAPTER TWENTY-SEVEN
THE DEFINING ISSUE

SPEAKER OF the Assembly Howard Doanes was California's most powerful legislator. When Larry was Lieutenant Governor and presided over the State Senate, he'd considered Doanes peculiar but honorable. They'd been out of touch since Larry became Acting Governor, and Doanes's call to Ted Roffman came out of the blue.

"Any idea what he wants?" Larry asked.

"None," Ted replied. "But under the Truth in Packaging Law, this guy should wear an eye patch and fly a skull and crossbones flag. If you seem eager to meet, he'll drive a harder bargain so I scheduled his appointment for the day after tomorrow."

Two days later, Ted showed Doanes into Larry's office. Once again Larry was amazed to see how little attention the man paid to his appearance. Bushy-browed, he wore black shoes with brown laces and carried a scuffed-up, hard-shelled, tan pigskin briefcase. His oversized body was encased in a baggy tweed suit.

"What I have to say is for your ears only," he said, limply shaking Larry's hand and staring at Ted.

"Would you like some coffee?" Larry asked

"With cream and sugar," Doanes replied.

"Ask Lois Brady to bring us some coffee, will you please, Ted?"

"We should've had a meeting back when you became acting governor," Doanes began, snuffing out his cigarette, "but I got all proud and decided it was your place to ask for my help—not my place to offer it. Oh, well. No harm done.

"If there's a next time, remember the line from *Alice in Wonderland* that says, 'Begin at the beginning and go on 'til you come to the end; then stop.' That's good advice, but you started in the middle, and when you got to the end, you didn't stop."

"Which means?" Larry asked.

"To begin at the beginning, you should've consulted the Legislature before sending so many armored personnel carriers into South Central. To stop when you came to the end, you should've sent the Guard home long ago."

Lois Brady knocked on the door, opened it, and delivered a tray with a pot of coffee, cups, spoons, cream, sugar, and artificial sweetener.

"Your State of the State speech to the Legislature last month," Doanes continued after Lois left, "had Hallie Martin's fingerprints all over it. However, you delivered it like you meant every word, and I believe you did. That's why I'm asking you to withdraw your request for Y.P.P. funding rather than have it denied, which it will be."

"I'd rather lose," Larry replied, "than not try."

"You've got a lot to learn about politics," Doanes said, slurping his coffee. "It's not *whether* you try, but *when*. You'll never get financing while the National Guard is in South Central. John Q. would see that as rewarding bad behavior, and elected representatives like to keep him happy.

"If South Central remains peaceful after the Guard withdraws, I'll help you get the funding you want."

"Why are you so opposed to having the Guard in South Central?"

"Military troops," Doanes said, "aren't an instrument for social change. Never have been. Never will be."

"General MacArthur's American troops in occupied Japan after World War II oversaw the transformation of an entire nation," Larry pointed out.

"You oughta stay away from that analogy. It gives your opponents the opportunity to suggest that you see South Central's residents as a conquered people." Doanes sighed. "Are we off the record here?"

"Absolutely."

"All African-Americans want is equality, which we in the Legislature keep finding excuses to dole out in small increments. Most of us have no idea of what their lives are like, but we want to be thanked for giving them what should already be theirs.

"This soon after the Carl Young Riot, there's no support for dipping into the public treasury to help a race many think gets more special consideration than it should. I used to think Blacks could have at least said thank you after we gave them some of the rights we had at birth. Now I believe race is *the* defining issue by which history will judge us."

The following morning, Larry withdrew his request for state funding.

CHAPTER TWENTY-EIGHT
MIXED COUPLES

BACK FROM his honeymoon, Michael Bridges toured South Central for the first time since he and Regina Butler had married. During his previous visits, guardsmen had been relaxed, helmet straps unbuckled, assault rifles slung loosely over their shoulders, talking with civilians and lavishing attention on children.

While he'd been in Hawaii, twelve guardsmen had been shot dead. Now the soldiers patrolled in groups, helmets and bulletproof vests strapped in place, rifles at the ready. Their grim, businesslike officers waved away civilians who tried to approach them.

There had even been a well-publicized incident during which White guardsmen had refused to patrol with Blacks.

While stopped at a traffic light near a school playground, Michael saw a National Guard Humvee pull over a Red Ford Mustang on the other side of the intersection ahead. His view was blocked as an LAPD motorcycle officer held up traffic while fully loaded National Guard troop trucks sped past.

Bridges turned on his rental car's air conditioner. Through a gap in the convoy, he saw the Mustang's driver, a Black teenage boy, get out and stand on the sidewalk.

After the last truck sped through the intersection, the officer who'd held up traffic followed. Across the intersection, guardsmen were searching the Mustang. Its doors and trunk were wide-open and the rear seat—now detached—was upside down on the sidewalk.

Bridges drove across the intersection, parked, and watched guardsmen search the Mustang's trunk and toss its contents willy-nilly on the sidewalk.

"No weapons, sir," one said.

As the Sergeant and his men climbed into their Humvee, Bridges hurried toward them.

"Hold it right there," the Sergeant ordered. "You're close enough."

"Evidently that boy didn't do anything wrong," Bridges said, stopping. "Shouldn't your men put his car back the way it was?"

"What business is that of yours?" the Sergeant asked as the Humvee pulled away from the curb.

"What reason did those guys give for stopping you?" Michael asked the boy.

"They said a Mustang like mine was involved in a shoot-out with one of their patrols last night." He turned his back toward a White girl standing nearby and lowered his voice. "Their real reason for stopping me was because they saw her in my car."

"My name is Michael Bridges. I have connections in the Guard. If what you say is true, they'll punish those guys."

"He's telling the truth," the girl said, coming closer. "They said things about my taste in boyfriends and told Tibeau they didn't like niggers polluting their gene pool."

"Did they use that word... niggers?"

"More than once," the girl replied, crossing her heart.

As a teenager, Bridges had been stopped by a White policeman for a minor traffic violation. Initially the officer had said he'd only issue a verbal warning. After noticing the

White girl in the front passenger seat, however, he'd written a ticket for worse than Bridges had done.

—ꟿ—

That afternoon at General Nelson's headquarters, Bridges told Tony Jackson what he'd witnessed.

"I'm surprised," Tony said, "that's not on the news already."

"It will be soon enough," Bridges told him. "There were plenty of witnesses. It'll be a major story."

"Is Tibeau willing to file a complaint?" Tony asked.

"Long as he doesn't have to testify against the Guard. After what happened today, he's afraid of you guys. I'll file the complaint."

"No. That would mean a court-martial and negative publicity that'll portray the Guard as racists. Don't go away. I'll find out who was patrolling that area. Their names will be on the duty roster."

—ꟿ—

The morning patrols came in at noon. Michael Bridges pointed out the eight soldiers he'd seen with Tibeau. Tony Jackson marched them to the hallway outside General Nelson's office and lined them up, backs to the wall.

"Those three didn't participate," Bridges said, pointing to guardsmen who'd watched Tibeau's hazing with disapproval.

"You're free to go," Tony informed them, "after you give your statements."

Military policemen took them to interrogation rooms.

"Evans," Tony snapped at the Sergeant in charge of the patrol. "This morning did you have occasion to stop a red

Mustang driven by a young Black man accompanied by a White girl?"

"Yes, sir, but—"

"The young man tells me," Tony interrupted, "you searched his car because a vehicle of that description was involved in a shooting last night. No such incident has been reported. Explain that without insulting my intelligence or I'll assign you to patrol the worst gang area in South Central with a Confederate flag tied to your Humvee's antenna.

"Or ..." Tony paused for effect, "you can avoid any further punishment by voluntarily apologizing and making amends."

"What kinds of amends?" the Sergeant asked suspiciously.

"This afternoon—in the presence of reporters and the young man and woman you insulted—wash and wax his car, dress the tires, polish the chrome, clean the windows inside and out, and vacuum the interior."

"That's it?" Sergeant Evans asked.

"Unless you do something else stupid," Tony replied.

Residents near Mary McLeod Bethune School came out to watch when the news media camera crew arrived and students came outside to assemble on the playground. They watched a CANG troop truck unload five guardsmen and two Military Policemen.

"We shouldn't do this in front of these kids," one of the M.P.s told Tony. "That'll decrease their respect for the Guard."

"What respect?" Tony asked. "They saw what happened. We'll never convince them we're perfect. The best we can do is to prove we correct our mistakes."

By the time the waxing was complete, the spectators were talking and laughing. Tony's quick thinking had salvaged the Guard's favorable reputation ... for the moment at least.

CHAPTER TWENTY-NINE
THE MADRASAS

TONY JACKSON'S effort to locate the Islamic fundamentalist *madrasa* spewing hatred in South Central had made little progress the day he took one of its students—a gang member named Kamasi—hiking on Mt. Whitney.

Today, Tony was trying again during their trip to Sequoia National Park's Giant Forest, home to five of the world's ten largest trees. There, as they admired the General Sherman, reputed to be the largest tree of all, Kamasi let it slip that the *madrasa* he attended was in a warehouse.

Late the following afternoon, back in South Central, Tony stopped his Humvee to talk with a National Guard patrol. As he got out, something slammed into his chest. Normally his Kevlar vest would've stopped a bullet, but this one was armor-piercing.

The CANG patrol quickly stormed the building from which the shot had been fired. When they came back outside empty-handed, their medic informed them that South Central had lost the man who was arguably its best friend.

—๛—

Gene Rice paused, then passed along the news of Tony's death in the gymnasium from which he'd broadcast his radio show for the last ten days. A girl on stage named Amira buried her face in her hands and sobbed.

"Did you know him?" Rice asked gently.

"I was there," she replied, "the day he made fools of those Nazis at Ted Watkins Park. Who killed him?"

"No matter who pulled the trigger," Rice said, "it was hatred that killed him, and I believe the killer may have been encouraged to hate in a *madrasa*. Does anyone here know anything about one of those in South Central?"

"One of my friends goes to a *madrasa*," Taye Sanford said. "But I don't know anything about it."

"I'd like to invite his teacher to appear on my show," Rice said.

When Rice followed up a few days later, Taye reported that the teacher in question wasn't interested.

Gene Rice had long theorized he might be part-German because he had the stereotypical Teutonic temperament. Once he established a routine, it didn't vary. As he was doing tonight, he always drove home after his show along the same route, beginning on the 101 Freeway North.

Shortly before the predictable stop-and-go traffic, he exited onto surface streets, then returned to the 101 where traffic was moving again.

Tonight, patchy fog held him below normal speed. Shortly before Thousand Oaks, Rice turned off the freeway and went west on a two-lane road through coastal mountains. The fog thickened as he neared the ocean.

Not far from the coastal highway he turned onto a narrow, winding uphill road. Even with his low beams, light from his headlights was reflected back at him. His wipers smeared the oily mist on his windshield, blurring his view. Following the broken white center line, he gave it his complete attention.

Halfway up the mountain, he sensed something was wrong and slammed on the brakes. His car slid to a stop. The sound he heard was all wrong. It wasn't the squeal of rubber on asphalt, but the grinding of tires sliding in dirt.

Rice peered through the windshield, then opened the car door and leaned out into the chilly fog for a better view. His car was on the road's shoulder, at the top of a sheer drop off. Mysteriously, what appeared to be the white center line was only two feet to his left.

A pair of headlights lit up and a pick-up came at Rice's car from behind. Anticipating a collision, he pushed the brake pedal harder. The truck's bumper crashed into his trunk.

Rice's car slid forward and the truck's engine roared as if protesting the added strain of pushing a vehicle being held back by all-wheel brakes. Then the hood dipped toward the canyon below and the car went over the edge, beginning a slow somersault as it plunged downward.

The pick-up backed away from the edge of the precipice, and three men got out. One headed down the road, picking up pieces of black rubber that had hidden the road's broken, white center line. A second man gathered white rubber strips. Identical to the real center line, they'd guided Rice's car toward the cliff.

By the time they threw their rubber strips into the pick-up's bed, Muhammad Nasheed had touched up the dirt shoulder with a broom. All that was left were two skid marks, showing where Gene Rice had left the road, apparently after losing his bearings in the fog.

Rice's death would look like an accident. No one would suspect a connection between it, Tony Jackson's murder, and a Muslim madrasa in an old warehouse.

—m—

After sleeping on the couch in his Sacramento office, Larry had shaved and finished the rest of his morning routine when Darth Vader unlocked the door and let himself in.

Larry was in the lunchroom, humming and pouring a cup of coffee.

"Judging by your good mood," Vader said, "you haven't heard the bad news. Gene Rice was killed in a freak auto accident last night."

Larry felt as if his windpipe had collapsed. He cleared his throat repeatedly.

"He ran off the road in heavy fog," Vader continued, "and went over a cliff. The California Highway Patrol says it was an accident, but it's a hell of a coincidence that he and Tony Jackson were working together and died violent deaths within days of one another."

"Let's take a look at the accident scene," Larry suggested.

—m—

After landing in Los Angeles, Darth Vader drove Larry toward Thousand Oaks at a consistent five miles an hour above the speed limit. Near Gene Rice's house, they stopped behind a Highway Patrol car on a sharp, narrow curve where yellow accident scene tape was strung between stakes to block off a section of the road's shoulder.

Vader stopped behind the CHP vehicle just as its flashing caution lights came on. By the time the driver stepped out with a camera, Larry and Vader were walking toward him.

"Why the pictures?" Vader asked. "Does CHP suspect foul play?"

"No." The photographer stared at Vader's massive size. "The investigating officers ruled that this was an accident, but it's CHP policy to take photos when there are fatalities and no witnesses."

While the officer took pictures of the road, the shoulder, and the tire tracks leading to the cliff, Darth Vader stood nearby, deep in thought.

"Why do you suppose the tire tracks are blurry where they leave the asphalt, then perfectly clear, then blurry again?" Vader asked.

"Rice was probably pumping his brakes," the Highway Patrol photographer speculated.

"Do you mind," Vader asked Larry, "if I call a friend at the FBI and have him send someone to make plaster casts of these tire tracks?"

"The FBI doesn't investigate automobile accidents," the photographer declared.

"They do if it's a murder," Vader said. "I'll stay here and make sure nothing happens to the tracks before the FBI gets here."

Two days later, Larry called the FBI's Los Angeles office and inquired about their analysis of Gene Rice's accident. His call was transferred to Lanier Clark, the section chief.

"Those tracks," Clark reported, "clearly show that Mr. Rice's car stopped short of the cliff and was shoved the rest of the way with its brakes engaged. We got an excellent casting of a tire on the vehicle that pushed him. It was a pick-up truck. I'll keep you informed of our progress. In the meantime get Darth Vader some help. You may be in danger."

CHAPTER THIRTY
EMILY

The garage door opener wasn't working when Larry got home that night. Taking two steps at a time, he hurried up the marble staircase to the front door, opened it, and stepped inside. He'd taken Emily to the airport. If she was home, she'd have come in a taxi.

Once inside, Larry began looking and made it all the way to the master bedroom without finding Emily. He did an about-face, hurried down the hall, and ducked into her office. Picking up the telephone, he dialed Michael Bridges' office in L.A.

"She spent the day at Jefferson High School," Bridges reported. "I assume she went to the airport from there."

Larry searched the house again, glancing into each room and calling her name. On his way through the kitchen, he popped a cookie into his mouth and was still chewing it when he found Emily in a chair that couldn't be seen from the living room's entryway. Though it was dark outside, she hadn't turned on a light.

"Hi," she greeted lifelessly.

"What's wrong?" he asked, turning on a floor lamp and seeing her bloodshot, red-rimmed eyes.

"We had a new volunteer today," Emily said. "She's a well-to-do White lady from Palos Verdes Peninsula who hasn't been around Black people much and is extremely uncomfortable around them.

"After recess, a girl—all hot and sweaty—brushed up against her arm, and she wiped it off very thoroughly."

Larry untied his shoes, kicked them off, and sat down beside Emily.

"On my way to the airport," she continued, "I got lost in a neighborhood where every house had iron grills in front of the windows and doors.

"A group of Black men on a corner yelled at me. I locked the doors, and tried to keep going, but one of them jumped in front of my car. I was so frightened that I considered running over him. Another man came up to the driver's side window and asked me to roll it down. I told him to talk through it.

"It turned out I was going the wrong way on a one-way street. Those men were trying to warn me, and I considered running one of them down, which wouldn't have occurred to me if they were White."

Larry felt the relief that came when his dentist stopped drilling.

"Don't beat yourself up, Emily," he said. "You're the least prejudiced person I've ever known."

"Black people never get to stop thinking about race," Emily said wearily. "How often does one call a talk show to discuss some other subject? When Lewis Franklin said: 'everything in America comes down to race,' it was the only time I ever disagreed with him. I can name lots of things that have nothing to do with race: farm subsidies, airline safety, the environment.

"Under normal circumstances, race seldom crosses my mind, but Black people think about it every minute of every day. When kidnap victims or prisoners of war are released, we provide counselors to help them deal with the trauma. But instead of therapy, Blacks are told to pull themselves up by their bootstraps. God. Many of those in South Central don't have boots."

Emily stood. Larry followed suit, then reached out to hug her. She put her hands against his chest and shook her head, then changed her mind and let him. She needed him to comfort her after almost intentionally running over a good Samaritan on a one-way street in South Central.

CHAPTER THIRTY-ONE
ANOTHER CALL FROM THE PRESIDENT

"GENERAL NELSON needs experts in urban guerrilla warfare to train his men," Larry told John Ainscourt, the Marine General assigned to South Central. "He thinks you're the man for the job."

"I hate to turn down that request," Ainscourt said. "But it's one thing to put down a riot and another to train soldiers to conduct urban warfare against American citizens. If I do that, I'll wind up testifying before Congress."

Later, Larry received a call from Allan Ripley.

"Governor Winslow," the President began, "the Vice President will be in California next week. While there, he's going to take a look at the situation in South Central."

"When will he get here?" Larry asked.

"His itinerary isn't firm yet. To be honest, I don't understand why ten thousand guardsmen find it difficult to handle rabble like those gangs."

"Someone has done an excellent job of instructing them in urban guerrilla warfare," Larry said. "The Guard has no such schooling, and its general was turned down when he asked for trainers from the Marines' urban warfare unit."

"I see where you're headed," Ripley said sternly, "and it seems to me that this request should come from General Nelson and go directly to General Ainscourt."

"General Ainscourt already turned us both down. If you're satisfied with the Vice President's report, I'm hoping you might give General Ainscourt a call."

"Under no circumstances," the President said, "will I ask a general to have U.S. soldiers trained for military operations against American citizens inside the United States."

"I understand, Mr. President. Thank you for calling." Larry hung up, and called Ted Roffman into his office.

"President Ripley is sending Vice President Scofield on a fact-finding mission to South Central," he began. "My guess is that he's getting ready to federalize the Guard and order them out of South Central."

"Naw. He's looking for a way to placate his liberal supporters," Roffman replied. "He's too good a politician to stand the Guard down right after the Chief of the Los Angeles Police Department predicted law and order would collapse without them. When's Scofield coming?"

"The President didn't know for sure."

"My guess," Roffman said, "is he'll come soon and before he touches base with you, he'll meet with California's movers and shakers. Scofield's a master of every dirty trick in the book. If I had my way, I'd lay him and Ripley side by side and have Evel Knievel's son jump them with a D-8 bulldozer."

The day before the Vice President was to tour South Central, he called Larry.

"I'm in Sacramento," he said. "Would you, Ted Roffman, and Michael Bridges like to have lunch with my aides and me?"

"Absolutely."

"Do you like French cuisine?"

"Who doesn't?"

"Let's meet at Waterboy Restaurant on Capitol Avenue at noon," Scofield suggested.

After calling Ted's office on the intercom, Larry said, "We're having lunch with the Vice President at noon. I'll meet you and Michael in the lobby in thirty minutes."

Traffic was unusually heavy, giving Ted time to tell Larry what he'd learned about the Vice President's visit so far.

"This morning," he began, "Scofield met with Speaker of the Assembly Howard Doanes and Governor Webster at Mercy General Hospital. It looks like you were right. He's lining up support for having President Ripley federalize the Guard and withdraw it."

Larry, Ted, Michael, and Darth Vader were late for their appointment when they walked out of the elevator into Waterboy Restaurant. The maître d' showed them to a table—off by itself—where two men were eating salad.

Calling attention to Larry's tardiness, Scofield stood and said, "We're on a tight schedule, so we had the waiter bring our salads."

The waiter took their orders: duck breast with brown butter gnocchi and bacon braised endive for Vice President Scofield; steak tartare for his aide; pork shoulder for Larry; and a Waterboy deluxe cheeseburger for Ted.

"If we'd known you were in town," Larry said after the waiter left, "we'd have provided you a car and driver."

"I wanted to see how you do things when you don't know you're being watched." Scofield chuckled as if his remark was a joke.

Holding his temper, Roffman came up with one of his trademark stories that make a point.

"Yesterday Costa Rica's government allowed its people to carry away baskets of turtle eggs from the beaches. The resulting protest from environmentalists was silenced when more female turtles came and buried their eggs above the existing nests. For some as yet unknown reason, Costa Rica gets more baby turtles that way."

"And your point is ... ? Vice President Scofield asked, eyes narrowing.

"That things aren't always what they seem, and you should get the facts before you make accusations."

"Tomorrow," Larry told Scofield as they ate, "I'd like to take you to the burial service at Forest Lawn Cemetery for Tony Jackson. He's a guardsman murdered by South Central's gangs. Nothing I can think of will give you a better idea of how South Central's residents feel about the Guard."

"Is Jackson the corporal I read about in *Time* magazine?" Scofield asked.

Larry nodded.

The Vice President picked up his starched linen napkin, touched it to his mouth, and continued, "He struck me as interesting. Is his Young People's Project doing as much good as *Time* reported?"

"You can ask people at his funeral tomorrow," Larry replied.

"Where is his service being held?"

"At the Simon Rodia Towers."

"Is that a hotel?" the Vice President asked.

Roffman snorted.

"No," Larry replied. "It's a collection of seventeen world-famous towers, started back in the 1920s by an Italian immigrant who spent thirty years building them, without machinery or helpers.

"The best-known is almost as tall as the Statue of Liberty, made of structural steel and wire mesh, and covered with mortar. People in Watts call it their Eiffel Tower."

"Will we be safe there?" Scofield asked.

For years, increases in Scofield's popularity had brought corresponding rises in Ted's blood pressure. Unable to contain himself, he barged into the conversation.

"You and the Governor," he said, "are telling people that South Central will be safe with the Guard gone. In that case it stands to reason that it should be the safest place on earth with hundreds of guardsmen there, paying Tony their last respects."

Glancing at his watch the Vice President announced, "I have other meetings scheduled today. Why don't you folks fly to Los Angeles with me on Air Force Two tomorrow morning? We'll continue this conversation then."

CHAPTER THIRTY-TWO
DEBATE ON AIR FORCE TWO

AT 6:00 AM the next morning Air Force Two, a modified Boeing 757, took off from Sacramento International Airport. Reporters sat in its rear compartment, an area similar to the interior of a commercial passenger plane.

In the Vice President's private section, seats were arranged in clusters to facilitate conversation. The leather-covered chairs, mahogany tables, and plush blue curtains reminded Larry of the luxurious railway cars that transported America's millionaires in the early 1900s.

The engines' roar diminished as the pilot reduced the rate of climb.

"We'll be in Los Angeles soon, Mr. Vice President," Larry said. "Would you like to have me go over today's itinerary?"

"I went over it last night," Scofield replied briskly.

Larry's further attempts to make polite conversation were equally unproductive.

—~—

After landing at Los Angeles International Airport, Air Force Two taxied past rows of private planes that were tied down on the runway, then stopped near stretch limousines, motorcycle cops, and squad cars.

Mayor Dean Payne was waiting on the tarmac at the foot of a portable stairway. After introductions, Secret Service agents took Scofield and his entourage to one of the limousines.

Larry and his party were escorted to another vehicle. Darth Vader sat in its rear-facing seat, where he could watch Ted Roffman, Larry, Emily, and Michael Bridges in the third seat, facing him. The driver locked the doors with a master switch.

"Don't unlock the doors until I say it's safe," a Secret Service agent with a badge that said Agent Dodge ordered. "And don't lean forward so people outside can see you."

He took a small radio from his inside coat pocket and put it on the seat between himself and Darth Vader.

The limousines began rolling, single file with two squad cars out front, two behind, and a line of motorcycles on either side. This formation crossed the runway at sixty miles an hour and swept through a gate onto a street usually reserved for airport personnel.

It left the huge airport through a second gate, which security guards unlocked and swung open at the last minute. Flashing red lights cleared the way as the limousines sped down a street temporarily cleared of traffic, and up an on-ramp.

After merging into the 105 Freeway's slow lane, the procession crossed all four lanes of traffic with military precision, allowing no outside vehicles into its ranks. By the time the motorcade reached the fast lane, it was at the speed limit and still accelerating.

After exiting into Watts, the motorcade approached a National Guard barricade. Three guardsmen moved it, giving access to Wilmington Avenue, which was closed to other traffic. Going north, all intersecting streets were blocked with wooden barriers.

The radio next to Dodge buzzed. He picked it up, held it to his ear like a phone, and listened.

"There's heavy pedestrian traffic congesting the street ahead," he told his fellow passengers.

Leaning forward, Larry looked out the side window.

"Sit back please, Governor Winslow," Dodge ordered.

Larry felt the car brake sharply. Through the windshield he saw pedestrians, men in their finest suits and women in their Sunday dresses, all with black armbands. He felt Emily slide closer and sensed her uneasiness. Folding his arms across his chest, he touched her shoulder.

CHAPTER THIRTY-THREE
THE SIMON RODIA TOWERS

WITH PEDESTRIANS within two feet of the Vice President's motorcade on both sides, the limousines were in uncomfortably tight quarters. Ahead, the crowd slowly parted to let them through, then filled in behind, as if they were in an air bubble traveling through water.

Larry saw the Simon Rodia Towers ahead and was duly impressed. Their construction by one man had required a rare combination of creativity, artistry, engineering, and stamina.

His attention was drawn to the pick-up truck ahead as it pulled into a parking space. Two brown-skinned boys got out. Under the watchful eyes of soldiers standing guard, they secured chairs to the top of a picnic table in their vehicle's bed and put up a sign: 'Prime Viewing for Fifty Dollars.'

When one saw a teenaged Black girl trying to push an elderly lady in a wheelchair over a curb, he helped her turn the chair around and pull it up on the sidewalk.

"Thank you," she said, smiling. "I don't know why grandma insisted on coming. She won't see anything with all these people standing in front of her."

"My friend and I can lift her into one of the chairs on our truck," the boy offered.

"We can't afford fifty dollars," the girl told him.

"No charge," the boy said impulsively. "We'll put her in the shade until the service starts."

Later, school teachers draped a tall amphitheater railing with red, white, and blue cloth. Larry read one of the notes pinned there. It read: 'Good-bye Tony. See you in Heaven.'

Parking spaces reserved for the motorcade had been overrun by spectators on foot. As Larry helped Emily out of the limousine, Agent Dodge walked up to a National Guard Sergeant.

"Why," he demanded, "aren't these parking spaces open?"

"We figured we'd clear them when you got here," the Sergeant explained.

"Can the cars be parked elsewhere?" Larry asked Dodge.

"No. We need them readily available, in case of an emergency."

"If you force these folks to move, they'll wind up too far away to see or hear the service," Larry pointed out.

By then, a television cameraman was filming their discussion and Vice President Scofield stepped in.

"It's okay," he told Dodge. "Park the cars as close to here as you can. We'll be fine."

Ted Roffman rolled his eyes and whispered to Larry, "Scofield was quiet as a church mouse, until television cameras showed up."

Standing in hot sunshine, the limousines' occupants were immediately surrounded by Secret Service agents. Moments later, Larry slipped through the protective ring of men in blue suits and made his way to General Nelson and Devon Washington, Tony Jackson's best friend.

"You two keep getting pushed farther from the stage," he said. "Why don't you sit with us?"

Larry introduced General Nelson to the Vice President, then proceeded with other introductions.

"This is Michael Bridges and his fiance, Regina Bradley," he began. "Michael was Tony's assistant. He'll be running the Y.P.P. from now on."

"I know Mr. Bridges well." The General patted Michael's shoulder. "To his credit, he was unfazed when the media gave Tony credit for many of his ideas. He's focused on doing good work—not on getting praised. That makes him the right man for the job."

Larry's attention was drawn to four men wearing clerical collars and he recognized Calvin Wilson—Carl Young's right hand man—who was becoming as prominent as his slain boss had been.

"You've done commendable work here in South Central," Wilson said as they shook hands. Turning to the Vice President he added, "The night Reverend Young gave his last speech, Governor Winslow was there. The Reverend accurately predicted he'd help the Black community, and he has. He's given us the gift of hope."

Newsman Brian Waterman asked Vice President Scofield for an interview and escorted him to where KTLA's cameraman waited.

"Waterman is asking questions that emphasize what you're accomplishing in South Central," Ted told Larry quietly.

"You think?" Larry asked.

"I'm sure. I can tell when Scofield's eating crow and pretending to like it."

Later Brian Waterman hurried over to Larry and quietly said, "If you'll join my interview with the Vice President, I'll feed you some big, fat pitches you can hit a mile."

"Some other time, " Larry replied. "This is Tony Jackson's day."

CHAPTER THIRTY-FOUR
WHY I LEFT THE NAZIS

LETICIA JACKSON had meticulously planned her husband's memorial service. She'd ruled out all religious aspects because Tony—disappointed with his church's failure to join the Black movement—had been 'cutting out the middle man and dealing directly with God,' as he called it.

"I want you to be the keynote speaker," Leticia had told Larry. "You gave him an opportunity no one else would have."

At Larry's suggestion, Leticia had asked Tony's father, Antonio, to do the honors instead.

That invitation had brought tears to the old man's eyes. He'd come to the Simon Rodia Towers in the Vice President's limousine. As he got out, his deeply lined face showed the effort it took for him to perform what should have been a relatively simple task.

Antonio had chronic arthritis which required him to use aluminum crutches. Instead of supporting him beneath the armpits, they gripped his forearms with leather bands.

Stooped and twisted, Antonio bore little resemblance to the young man wrapped in an American flag in the Pulitzer-Prize-winning photograph that hung in Emily's home office. It was taken as he marched across the Edmund Pettus Bridge during the 1965 Voting Rights March in Alabama.

"Glad you could come," Larry greeted him. Seeing that the old man didn't dare let go of his crutches, Larry touched Antonio's shoulder rather than offer a handshake.

"Have you been to the Simon Rodia Towers before?" he asked.

"A few times with Tony," Antonio replied. "When he was in high school, this was his favorite place. He said it proves how much one man can accomplish if he applies himself."

"You raised an extraordinary human being."

"When born, he was a bag of elbows, shoulder blades, and knees, but he turned out pretty well. You can't imagine how it hurts to have lost him, but it would have been far worse to never have known him."

—∾—

The Watts Towers Amphitheater was an open-air facility that hosted musical and theatrical performances. The plaza in front was packed when Larry helped Antonio to the stage and the fire department shut down access because there were no more seats available.

Leticia Jackson had asked Vice President Scofield to say a few words, and had warned him not to say anything even remotely critical of the National Guard.

Scofield's aide approached Leticia, leaned over, and whispered to her. She listened, shook her head, and sent the aide on his way with a firm, "No."

Ted Roffman overheard the aide's question and couldn't resist offering his opinion.

"Change your mind," he told Leticia gently. "If Scofield wants Tony's father with him at the microphone, say yes."

"Why?" Leticia challenged. "That'll make him look better than he deserves."

"More likely," Ted replied, "it will show him for what he really is. There's no time to explain. Trust me."

Leticia walked over to the Vice President and reluctantly told him, "On second thought, it would be fitting for Tony's father to be onstage with you."

Leticia sent her son to deliver a note to the master of ceremonies.

After a quick glance, he announced, "Ladies and gentlemen, please welcome Roger Scofield, Vice President of the United States, and Tony Jackson's father, Antonio."

Guardsmen—side-by-side in blue uniforms, white belts, and gleaming silver helmets—marched onstage. At their center Antonio Jackson wore a t-shirt that said: 'Danger! Educated Black Man.'

Forgetting himself and smiling despite the occasion's somber nature, Scofield rushed to the microphone, harvesting the applause. In his enthusiasm, he left Antonio Jackson and his escorts behind.

Not yet aware of how tactless this looked, Scofield compounded an initial bad impression by speaking while Tony's father was still coming across the stage. His speech sounded as if he'd given it—filling in the blanks with different names—at the funerals of every head of state who'd died while he was in office.

If he'd understood the Black psyche, he'd have been less controlled and more inspirational. His audience wanted to purge their sorrow—not listen to tired political platitudes.

When it was Antonio's turn, he took the microphone in both hands to steady himself.

"If you spent time around my son," he began in his frail voice, "you probably heard him say: 'Hatred is like acid. It destroys the container in which it's stored.' That saying symbolized his refusal to let the world embitter him. His positive attitude and optimism were gifts from God, and Tony wanted to pass them along to as many others as possible.

"For seventy years, the doors of Los Angeles were closed to Black people, and they were told to stay where they *belonged*.

Tony told South Central's sons and daughters that they *belong* anywhere they want to go, within reason.

"His Y. P. P. showed them how sweet life can be if they work hard and make good choices. He took poor and disadvantaged children away from joyless existences and showed them the good life."

—∾—

Called to the microphone by supporters who wouldn't take no for an answer, Leticia Jackson reluctantly obliged. Fighting back tears, she waited for her standing ovation to fade away and the audience to sit down.

"Thank you. Please don't allow Tony's dream to die with him," she managed before stage fright silenced her.

Leticia's regal bearing reminded newsman Brian Waterman of Jacqueline Kennedy after her husband, President John F. Kennedy, was assassinated in Dallas.

On his news broadcast that night, Waterman told his audience: "Leticia Jackson communicated more with her silence than the speakers did with their words."

—∾—

The Vice President and his aides had left for Air force Two and the flight back to Washington, D.C.

"I thought they'd never leave," General Nelson told Larry. "I have a surprise for you."

"A pleasant one, I hope," Emily said.

"That remains to be seen," Nelson replied. "Before today's service, my driver recognized one of the Nazis Tony humiliated at their rally in Ted Watkins Park. He told my driver the boys with him are his sons and he wanted them to see today's event.

"As a precaution, my driver had a guardsman take him and his boys into protective custody. We're about to turn him loose. Would you like to talk to him first?"

"I sure would," Emily said.

"I think you'll find him interesting," Nelson told her. "He told my driver he was bringing his sons so they could see how many people they'll have to fight if they copy what he was doing. His name is Rolf Becker. My driver says he seems intelligent and well-educated."

"I'd like to meet him, too," Tony's widow, Leticia, said. "My husband was happiest when getting people out of gangs, but this is the only time he ever got anyone to leave a White gang."

Under a stunning sunset, the General's car stopped at a 1960s style movie theater, not far from Simon Rodia Towers.

The glass-covered cases where posters had once advertised coming attractions were covered with plywood, and a sign on the butterscotch-colored art deco façade said: For Sale.

Hours earlier, the owner had been sweeping the sidewalk in front when General Nelson's driver asked if the theater had a room where the Guard could keep a man and two boys they had in protective custody.

Nelson led his group past the ticket window to the theater's glass doors and knocked on one with a coin. A man let them in, then led the way to the manager's office and unlocked the door.

Inside, Larry saw a checkerboard black and white tile floor, then a large, round clock with a red neon rim, and finally a worn-out couch where Rolf Becker and his sons sat, laughing.

"Hi," the older boy said cheerfully.

Larry had expected the Beckers to be sullen after hours in a locked room. They were far from it.

"This is Acting Governor Larry Winslow and his wife, Emily," General Nelson told Becker. "They'd like to talk with you, then my men will drive you home. This neighborhood can be dangerous for Caucasians at night."

"Is it true," Emily asked Becker, "you've had a change of heart about Black people?"

"About all people," Becker replied. "Can someone please take my boys elsewhere while we talk?"

Nelson's driver escorted Becker's sons from the room.

"Why this sudden goodwill toward the world?" Emily asked.

"It happened in stages." Becker paused. "For some reason I started feeling guilty about what's been done to people who aren't White. It's not right. Then one night I saw my boys walking around the house with rolled up pieces of paper, imitating me by pretending to smoke.

"I could see what would happen next, and I don't want them to smoke. Then last week, I overheard them talking about some Blacks at school and referring to them as niggers. That was why I brought them to Tony Jackson's memorial service."

Moments later, General Nelson's driver brought Leticia and Antonio Jackson into the room. They looked at Becker and he looked at the floor while Nelson introduced them.

Becker glanced at Leticia, looked away, and said, "Your husband made us look pretty bad that day at Ted Watkins Park. I admired the way he stuck up for those kids."

"He didn't stick up for them," Leticia declared. "He put them in a position where they could defend themselves with the truth."

"You told us how you stopped being a Nazi," Emily said. "How'd you start?"

"My father was a Marine who loved America so much he volunteered to fight in Vietnam. Later, he told me about a Saigon neighborhood where Black soldiers went on leave and didn't return to their units. Military Police wouldn't go after them without a combat team.

"Worse yet, many Blacks refused to fight. When on patrol they found places to hide and smoked dope. If Viet Cong went by, they and the Blacks ignored each other.

"One time my dad opened fire, forcing his men to defend themselves. Afterward, they warned him they weren't willing to die for a country that called them niggers. They threatened to kill him with a fragmentation grenade if he ever involved them in another firefight."

"That was called fragging," General Nelson said, "and it got more attention than it deserved. But the media overlooked it when disgruntled Whites did the same. Ninety-seven percent of Blacks who served in Vietnam were honorably discharged, twenty were awarded the Medal of Honor, and six thousand were killed in action."

CHAPTER THIRTY-FIVE
COMPETING WITH THE SOVIETS

ROLF BECKER filled a paper cup at the water cooler, then sat down again on the couch.

"I grew up in Oakland," he answered Larry's latest question. "Our neighborhood was more Black than White, and fights were common. I learned karate and usually gave better than I received, but I got sliced up a couple of times.

"It bothered me that Blacks seemed to be lazy. I worked as a carpenter and never saw one work hard. They were constantly asking us White guys to slow down and stop making them look bad. Out of spite, we'd speed up.

"I used to wonder what America would be like if we traded our Blacks for Germans or Englishmen. I didn't want the Soviet Union to get ahead of us because they worked harder."

"I worried about that, too," Larry said. "But I looked at America's competition with the Russians differently. I figured we should prove our ideals were more than window dressing by giving our Blacks the same rights we have."

"I believe that now," Becker returned. "Back then, however, I thought we treated them too well. Affirmative action gave them preference when it came to jobs and admission to colleges. I figured if they had a work ethic, they wouldn't need preferential treatment.

"One time on a job in the Oakland hills, a Black union official got all huffy because there were no Blacks working there. Our foreman told him we needed four framers.

"After two hours, the men he sent were laying under a tree, cooling off. An hour later they quit.

"When I became a Nazi, it was because a lot of Blacks carried knives in those days. I felt like I needed protection and I joined the Nazis without bothering to do the math."

"What math?" Larry asked.

"Joining a gang," Becker replied, "doesn't work the way it's advertised. Theoretically you have more people to protect you from enemies. In fact, however, you've added your fellow gang members' enemies to your list."

"I read a book you should enjoy," Emily told Becker. "It was written by a White man who dyed his skin so he could observe life in the deep South from a Black man's perspective.

"One night he went into a liquor store, and two rednecks with clubs chased him into the parking lot, where he hid in the bed of a pick-up truck. Its owner, a farmer, came out of the store with wine. Thinking he was dealing with a Black man, he covered the writer with a tarp to hide him.

"Down the road a ways, he stopped and invited his passenger to ride up front with him and his two sons. The boys gave him a hamburger and french fries, the only kindness a White person had shown him since he'd disguised himself.

"Trying to figure out what had made this man different, he asked a series of questions. The only remarkable thing he discovered was the farmer's extraordinary love for his sons. Does that remind you of your relationship with your sons?"

—m—

During their drive home that night, Larry told Emily, "I congratulate myself for having hired Michael Bridges, but I'm ashamed to admit that our relationship is typical. We work together, and after quitting time we go our separate ways.

"I had one Black friend before Tony's murder, and now I have none. Antonio Jackson must be excruciatingly lonely after his son's burial today. Let's take him out for a meal at his favorite restaurant."

"Don't be surprised if there are no other White people there."

"I'm counting on it," Larry said. "I've been concentrating on Black history when I should've been concentrating on Black people."

—~—

With Tony Jackson and Gene Rice dead, their killer brought his diary up-to-date.

'Without knowing who he's fighting or why,' Muhammad Nasheed wrote, 'Acting Governor Winslow has thwarted my every move. Eliminating him will be perilous, but I see no alternative other than to abandon my plan for South Central. That, of course, is out-of-the-question.

'If this man was more conservative, he would've advanced my cause by cracking down on the Carl Young riot and touching off the revolution for which I've worked. If he was more liberal, he'd have given me more space and the Black revolt would have succeeded.

'To defeat him, I have to make him think with his gut—not his brain—to say and do things motivated by anger, hatred, and the need for revenge. He clearly loves his wife. If I rape and kill her, it should put him over the edge and send him looking for revenge.

'She's a beautiful woman, so it will also be a pleasure.'

CHAPTER THIRTY-SIX
MYSTERY MAN

IN LARRY'S office the next morning, his private telephone rang. He answered and heard a voice, distorted by a synthesizer.

"I know who killed Gene Rice and Tony Jackson," the voice said. "I'll give you that information for two hundred thousand dollars."

"How will I know it's accurate?" Preparing to take notes Larry picked up his pen, held the phone to his ear with his shoulder, and asked, "When and where do you want to meet?"

"I prefer meeting with your wife."

"If you really have evidence pertaining to those murders and refuse to divulge it, you're an accessory after the fact and can be jailed for life."

"No threats, my friend. I insist on meeting with your wife."

"That's out of the question. Who's your second choice?"

The caller hung up.

The next morning, Emily was asleep when Larry brought her a tray with bacon, pancakes, pats of butter, a small pitcher of heated maple syrup, and a single lavender rose he'd cut in the garden and put in her pewter bud vase. He arranged her pillows so she could sit up, then unfolded the tray's legs, and placed it across her lap.

"Mmmmmm," she expressed her approval. "Your mom's high-protein pancakes."

Emily suffered from low protein, and his mother's recipe called for lots of cottage cheese and eggs.

"A man called my office today," Larry said, "and claimed he knows who killed Gene Rice and Tony Jackson. He demanded two hundred thousand dollars and won't give the information to anyone but you. If he really has that information, he'll call again."

"That's scary."

"Extremely," Larry agreed. "Let's get you safely hidden away and see if he calls again. Would you like to go to La Quinta for a week?"

La Quinta was a luxury resort near Palm Springs. They'd spent their second honeymoon and several anniversaries there in relaxed moods rarely experienced by such high-powered people.

"I'm ready to go," Larry said. "How long will it take you to finish breakfast and pack a suitcase?"

Sunday morning at La Quinta, the phone next to Larry's side of the bed rang. He answered on the second ring.

Ted Roffman apologized for calling so early.

"You just had another call from your mystery man," he continued. "The police couldn't trace his call, and I couldn't talk him out of meeting with Emily."

After Larry and Emily had showered and dressed, Darth Vader left the adjoining room and sat with them during breakfast in the restaurant.

Blowing along the desert floor, the tumbleweed paralleled the dirt road Larry was following. Round except for a prominent bulge, it rolled and hopped, rolled and hopped, like a child burning excess energy.

Larry and Emily had spent five glorious days at La Quinta. Other guests would've been surprised to know they'd been married for years. They seemed like lovers in the midst of a glorious affair.

Rather than read in the early mornings, as he did at home, Larry had been taking walks in the desert, leaving Vader to protect Emily. Alone in the silent moonlight, free of distractions, he was putting the finishing touches on a major change in strategy.

The wind shifted, and the tumbleweed that had kept Larry company for the last half-mile suddenly blew into his path. He kicked it.

—ꟺ—

Back in their room with Emily, Larry called Ted.

"I want you to arrange," he said, "for me to meet with Moshe Meier in secret."

"The Israeli counter-terrorism expert?" Ted asked. "I think he's a little controversial for our needs. The civil rights people will go nuts if we consult him. Not only that, but he commands a hefty fee and comes with a team of high-priced assistants. You'll never get the legislature to appropriate funds."

"I'll pay for him," Larry replied, "if he agrees to meet and lives up to his reputation."

—ꟺ—

Moshe Meier was a former Israeli general cashing in on his reputation by teaching defensive driving and otherwise training bodyguards. Ted contacted him at an international conference on terrorism in Mexico City.

The Israeli agreed to fly to Los Angeles and meet with Larry and General Nelson at the Radisson Hotel near the LAX International Airport. Darth Vader drove both of them to the hotel's secluded freight dock, where the concierge waited.

"The gentleman you're meeting," the concierge said quietly, "is waiting in a conference room."

He led them to the service elevator, stepped inside, and turned his key in a lock so the elevator would go all the way to the top floor non-stop.

When they got there, the concierge checked the hallway before guiding them to a conference room and handing Larry a key card.

"I'll be back when you're through," he said, pocketing his gratuity.

Larry asked Darth Vader to wait in the hall.

Meier was older than Larry expected, but his face was wrinkle free except for a few that fanned from the outside corners of his eyes.

Extending his hand, Larry said, "I'm Governor Winslow."

"I know," Meier responded in a heavily accented voice, "and this gentleman is Lieutenant General Edward Nelson of the California National Guard."

He opened a small trunk on the conference table, grabbed an electronic wand and checked the room for listening devices.

"Ted Roffman," he explained, "told me the Crips and Bloods have shown a remarkable talent for anticipating what the Guard will do next. They may be familiar with the art of electronic eavesdropping."

Next he took four devices from the trunk, extended their antennas, and set them on chairs he'd moved away from the conference table and placed in the middle of each wall.

"For the benefit of customs officials," he explained, "these look like radios, but they're state-of-the-art jamming devices."

"Thank you for coming so quickly," Larry began as he and Nelson sat down across from Meier.

"The United States is Israel's best friend," Meier said, opening a binder and looking down at it. "I'll be glad to help you at no charge. May I be brutally frank, General Nelson?"

"Absolutely," Nelson replied.

"It seems to me," Meier said, "you've underestimated your enemy. That's understandable since you have no intelligence gathering apparatus. As a result, you defend but don't attack. That will never work against your opponents, who are clearly determined, motivated, and well-financed."

"Our funding is severely limited," Nelson said.

"You can do a great deal without spending more than you are. For example, don't let the gangs choose the battlefield. Put them on their heels with preemptive strikes. Infiltrate their ranks and take away their safe havens. Are they popular with South Central's residents?"

"Adults despise the gangs," Nelson replied. "But many of their sons are gang members, so they're understandably reluctant to give us information."

"Gathering intelligence in South Central can't be more difficult than it is among Israel's enemies," Meier declared. "Information—like beautiful women—must be pursued. It won't walk up, sit in your lap, and kiss you."

"Civil rights in this country," Nelson said, "are different from those in the Middle East."

"I'm sorry if I've ruffled your pride," Meier said. "I'll be glad to show you what works, but then it's up to you."

"I think I'm giving you the wrong impression," Nelson told Meier. "I'm grateful for the opportunity to learn from the world's foremost anti-terrorist."

"In that case," Meier said. "I'll be glad to show you how to kill a lot more of your enemies than you are now."

The impact of those words was sobering to Larry. In his mind, he'd declared *war* on South Central's gangs. Then after using the word that describes mankind's most terrible activity, he'd used euphemisms in further discussions.

"Our primary objective," he said, "isn't killing."

"To win a guerrilla war," Meier countered, "you have to kill the enemy's men in far greater numbers than he kills yours. Conventional wisdom says an army needs a four-to-one manpower advantage to win a guerrilla war.

"But in South Central, the National Guard is outnumbered. The only way to overcome that is to make this war so painful your enemy decides his objectives aren't worth the cost.

"You have to give CANG the tools and authorization to hurt the gangs as grievously as possible. Anything less will be a terrible lack of respect for your men's lives. How many casualties has CANG taken so far?"

"Six dozen dead and twice that many wounded," Nelson replied. "I'm not a fan of kill ratio theories. In Vietnam, that ratio was as high as twenty-to-one in our favor, and we still lost."

"For one simple reason," Meier said. "The United States decided its objectives weren't worth the cost. If you feel that way about South Central, send the Guard home today and don't waste any more lives."

CHAPTER THIRTY-SEVEN
A GOOD GUEST

"How would you suggest we start?" Larry asked after a week of familiarizing Meier with South Central.

"By setting up an intelligence gathering network," Meier said. "With all the social programs being implemented by General Nelson's men, they must have plenty of friends in the community."

"We do," Nelson replied.

"I imagine most of them are male."

"That's correct."

"You'll find," Meier said, "that Black women are more likely to provide information. For one thing, they head up most single-parent households, making them deeply concerned about gangs. They also have more of a stake in the community because, in general, they're more educated and employable. They greatly outnumber Black males in professions like teaching and medicine.

"This higher status dates back to their days as slaves. Negro males were chained in their living quarters when not working, but the women could become servants in their masters' homes, often without much supervision."

"You've done your homework," Larry said. "I'm impressed. You come from another country yet have information and insight beyond that of most Americans."

"Not really," Meier said. "I read a book by a man named Lewis Franklin last night."

"How long can you stay?"

"As long as I'm of use. If you want, I'll bring Israeli commandos to teach your men urban guerrilla warfare."

"Should I send a formal request to Israel's government?" Nelson asked.

"Informal arrangements are less cumbersome," Meier said, "and less likely to wind up being leaked to the press or investigated by Congress. I'd like my presence here to be a secret for as long as possible. If the Crips and Bloods don't know CANG is learning new tactics, we can thump them a few times before they adjust."

"Who'll have overall command?" Nelson asked.

"You can overrule me at your discretion," Meier replied. "I'm a guest here, and I'll do my best to be a good one."

"What do you think of Moshe Meier so far?" Larry asked during his daily briefing with General Nelson.

"I like him," Nelson replied. "He's brilliant."

"That shouldn't be a surprise. Most researchers break the races down into Black, White, Hispanic, Asian, Middle Eastern, Indian, East Indian, and *others*. When those researchers conduct IQ tests, Asians do better than anyone else.

"However, in studies where these groups are broken down into their individual components, Jewish people outscore every other racial group. I guess that's why they win a stunning 22% of the Nobel Prizes while comprising only .2% of the world's population."

CHAPTER THIRTY-EIGHT
OWNING THE NIGHT

Moshe Meier's electronic counter-surveillance measures were puzzling to Guardsmen in South Central's encampments. They protested when relieved of smartphones and other devices that could be hacked. General Nelson's explanations fell on deaf ears. Meier's—on the other hand—were convincing.

"You've assumed the gangs are too primitive to use electronic surveillance," he told individual officers, one-by-one. "But I'm convinced they're using their drug profits to buy sophisticated eavesdropping equipment. That's how they know what you're going to do next."

Other preparations for the coming CANG offensive included assigning medics to every patrol, equipping helicopters as ambulances, and setting up operating rooms at Los Angeles hospitals.

On a modern battlefield, CANG could easily have outgunned the gangs, but in an urban area, the Guard had to forego the use of its most effective weapons. So Meier advised General Nelson to provide his men with other advantages.

Fast, agile armored vehicles were hidden in warehouses. Unmarked crates from other branches of the military brought state-of-the-art weapons: range finders, binoculars, body armor, night vision scopes, flares, and infrared cameras that took pictures in almost no light.

The Guard had been fighting in broad daylight. Now they were ready to own the night.

—ꟿ—

During its early days, Muhammad Nasheed's war on the Guard had brought only limited success. However, once the gangs knew exactly what the Guard would do next, their attacks had caused enough casualties to lower CANG's morale.

Flushed with success, Nasheed now underestimated his opponent. As he prepared to double the Crips' and Bloods' attacks on patrols, he didn't yet know he was up against a new tactician who specialized in night fighting.

—ꟿ—

Intended to keep terrorists out, Israel's security fence consisted of observation posts, anti-vehicle ditches, intrusion detection sensors, and razor wire. In heavily populated urban areas, it was a twenty-six-foot tall concrete wall that had all but eliminated suicide bombings.

At Israel's Tel Aviv checkpoint, Lieutenant Amir Barsky was investigating an attack that killed six of his country's soldiers. He'd established that Israeli Defense Forces, IDF, had let two Palestinians pass through even though they were on a terrorist watch list.

After arranging for all the checkpoint's computers to be linked to that list, Barsky kept his appointment at Israel's Ministry of Defense in Tel Aviv. In Defense Minister Shimon Ben Zeev's spartan office, he saluted and stood at attention.

"At ease," Ben Zeev commanded.

Barsky relaxed, feet apart, hands clasped behind his back.

The minister looked up from his desk and said, "The prime minister wants you and twenty elite commandos to fly to Los Angeles and train California's National Guard in urban warfare. This mission is top secret."

Indistinguishable from tourists and businessmen, Barsky and his commandos—seated here and there among hundreds of passengers—flew from Tel Aviv to Los Angeles on an El Al Airlines 747-400 jet.

They were met by female National Guard officers in civilian clothes and driven in an unmarked bus to a truck stop near Ontario. There they were joined by Graham Keyes, General Nelson's second-in-command. He thanked them for coming and ushered them aboard a chartered Greyhound bus that took them north.

In a huge, well-lit hangar at the Fort Irwin Military Reservation, the commandos sat in chairs on a stage while Barsky stood at a microphone and addressed a thousand guardsmen from South Central.

"Gentlemen," he began, "we're from the IDF, Israeli Defense Forces. For the next month, we'll have the honor of showing you some tactics for dealing with guerrillas in urban areas. During that time, you'll be housed in a barracks here and are to avoid all contact with the outside world.

"This afternoon, you'll be taken to a remote part of Fort Irwin where portable buildings have been arranged to resemble a typical urban area. You'll patrol it in groups of fifty. My men and I will attack you.

"You and we will wear electronic sensors that buzz and flash when a hit is scored by our specially equipped rifles. Every day, the portables will be rearranged so we can show you the dangers and opportunities inherent in different urban surroundings."

After Barsky's speech the Israelis were taken to their quarters, and General Keyes gave his men a speech he didn't want anyone else to hear.

"Our Israeli guests are accustomed to working with crack professional troops," Keyes said, standing where Barsky had. "Right now, they're probably wondering if they can do much with us weekend warriors.

"Inexperienced soldiers often die when they take their first misstep. But here at Fort Irwin, the only consequence of a blunder is that your sensor lights up and buzzes. Here you can learn from your mistakes and live to fight again.

"Within two weeks, I want you holding your own, and by the time your training ends I want you defeating our IDF guests at least half the time. Let's show them what we're made of!"

CHAPTER THIRTY-NINE
ALL-OUT RACE WAR

AS GUARD units trained at Fort Irwin, the Crips and Bloods formed the Federation of Gangs. Strengthened by this union, they began attacking CANG's patrols with large Wolf Packs. Fighting grew so intense that LAPD was forced to pull its men out of South Central.

After two weeks at Camp Irwin, Amir Barsky assembled the elite Guard units in the hangar where he'd lectured them when he'd arrived.

"Your fellow guardsmen," he told them, "are under heavy pressure in South Central, and you're more than ready to go to their rescue. Good luck."

—ꝏ—

As CANG's elite units returned to South Central, General Nelson and Moshe Meier met.

"How would you feel," Meier asked, "about doing something that makes you look naive for a while?"

"I'd like to hear more before I answer," Nelson replied, chuckling.

"Would you be willing to announce that the Guard's plan to win the war with the gangs will begin with a campaign to eliminate their graffiti?"

"Not even the Crips and Bloods will believe I'm *that* simple-minded."

"My guess is that they'll believe it because they'll want to."

That afternoon, Nelson's announced new strategy was ridiculed, publicly by politicians and privately by the Federation's leaders.

That afternoon, graffiti was painted over and television cameras recorded the so-called counterattack on the gangs. The next night, the Federation's taggers re-marked some of their territory, unaware that guardsmen—watching from roofs, abandoned houses, and parked vehicles—were making lists of their vehicles' license plate numbers.

After several nights, the Guard had a comprehensive list. Next CANG investigators interrogated the vehicle owners and then looked into the activities of their recent associates—and *their* recent associates.

When they found people with police records fraternizing with known criminals, they got warrants to use wiretaps.

By forming a Federation, the Crips and Bloods had increased their numbers but made themselves more vulnerable. Both gangs had once been composed of semi-autonomous sets, each with its own leader. But with a single chain of command, CANG's investigators could find one link, then connect it to another and another until they found and arrested the bosses.

"The Federation will soon be playing checkers," was Ted Roffman's assessment, "while the Guard plays 3D chess."

—⁂—

Fazul Abdallah was a mujahideen commander and largely responsible for running the Russians out of Afghanistan in early 1989. Sent to South Central at Muhammad Nasheed's request, he evaluated the Federation's deteriorating situation.

"The National Guard appears to be using Zionist tactics," he reported to Nasheed. "If they have Israeli advisors, I can show you how to defeat them."

In Lebanon in 2006, Abdallah's Hezbollah troops had fought the seemingly invincible Israeli Defense Force to a standstill, depriving the IDF of victory in battle for the very first time.

"I'm looking forward to the rematch," he told Nasheed.

—m—

Muhammad Nasheed had trained his lieutenants for years. Several were now in jail and the National Guard's intelligence unit had found links between them and him. Already they'd sealed his house, closed his school, and were searching for him.

Tomorrow the FBI would examine his home and school with a fine-tooth comb. If they found his diary, a booby trap would explode, killing the finder and destroying the computer's contents before they could be read.

To compensate for the Federation's setbacks, Fazul Abdallah recommended Nasheed expand his struggle into as many White neighborhoods as possible. With the battlefield enlarged, the Guard would be forced to protect a larger area and the Federation would again be able to choose battles where it had the advantage.

"By the time the country realizes what's happening," Abdallah said, "it'll be too late to stop you. You might even gain the support of Black Muslims, who still have the allegiance of the tens of thousands who participated in the Million Man March on Washington, D.C."

In 1995 that march had been an enormous, peaceful gathering of African-American men. Held on the National Mall,

it had been called for by Louis Farrakhan for the purpose of putting Black issues on America's agenda.

A national Black spokesman, Farrakhan had praised Adolf Hitler as 'a great man.' As his rhetoric became more radical, he'd prophesied the United States' downfall and threatened Whites with divine punishment if his demands for racial equality were ignored.

For Larry's fiftieth birthday, Emily had arranged a low-key event attended by his favorite people. When he came home that night she was seated on the couch with Tony Jackson's father, Antonio. As if posing for a photo, Ted Roffman and Michael Bridges were in front of the fireplace.

"Please don't get up," Larry said, gently placing his hands on Antonio's shoulders.

Greeting Ted and Michael, Larry ignored their outstretched hands and gave them back-slapping hugs.

"General Nelson couldn't be here tonight," Ted told Larry. "The Guard is fighting in some White neighborhoods outside South Central."

"What?" Larry exclaimed. "That's the last thing I expected. At lunch today, I asked Nelson to make plans for withdrawing his men."

"Do we have to talk about this right now?" Emily asked. "This is a birthday party."

She dialed a Chinese restaurant, ordered take out, and sent a taxi to pick it up.

"Asking Nelson," Larry said, "to prepare a withdrawal was a spur of the moment decision. Looks like this is a bad time for that."

"Why?" Antonio Jackson asked. "My heart would've broken if my Tony had been killed by the Guard while he was in a gang. Thank God for letting him live and salvage hundreds of now useful members of society from gangs. He'd be proud of that legacy. With the troops gone, it's possible the Y.P.P can can continue to recruit gang members."

"Since we," Bridges offered, "moved our headquarters to a safe location outside South Central, the number of turncoats has skyrocketed. There's no way to know for sure if it will be better to leave the Guard, pull them out, or reduce their numbers."

"There's another side to that coin," Ted Roffman said. "The Guardsmen have the gangs on their heels and are on the verge of finishing them off. But if they withdraw, the Federation could regroup and the Guard would be forced back into a more dangerous environment than it left."

"America has an obligation to help Blacks get on an even footing with its other citizens," Emily said. "I think the Guard should stay and help them do that."

When Ted and Michael left, none of the food Emily ordered had been touched.

She and Larry helped Antonio settle into their guest room.

"A lot of good points were made on both sides tonight," Emily said when they were in bed. "Have you decided what you're going to do?"

"My most important goal has been to get as many people as possible to leave gangs, and it still is. If I withdraw the Guard and the situation deteriorates again, I or my replacement could be forced to send them back into a far worse situation than they left."

CHAPTER FORTY
THE DIARY

WHEN LARRY called Moshe Meier to Sacramento, he was pleased with what the Israeli had accomplished, but not how he was doing it.

"You've done a remarkable job," Larry began when they were seated in his office.

"I get the impression," Meier said, "you're about to tell me to restrain my activities."

"How do you always know exactly where and when to have General Nelson set up ambushes? You're never wrong. Are you using some of your electronic gear to illegally tap telephones?"

"The Guard," Meier replied, "isn't taking people to court, where that kind of evidence is inadmissible. It's simply waiting for criminals at the scenes of intended crimes."

"You agreed not to violate our laws."

"Laws are supposed to protect good people," Meier said smoothly. "The way Americans sometimes interpret them, however, they hamper law enforcement at society's expense."

"Look. We've got the gangs on the run, and we can't afford to get caught breaking the law."

"With martial law in effect," Meier said, "we're not breaking the law."

"Not the letter of the law perhaps," Larry replied, "but its spirit. Phone taps invade people's privacy. If President

Ripley knew we're using them without getting warrants, he'd pull the Guard out and a majority of Americans would heartily approve."

—~—

When General Nelson's private phone rang, he checked his caller ID display, then answered.

"Governor Winslow I presume," he greeted.

"I've decided to change strategy," Larry began. "Effective immediately the Guard will discontinue offensive operations against the Federation, but will continue legally gathering intelligence."

—~—

"I'll never understand Americans," Moshe Meier said as Larry drove him to the airport. "You claim to deplore violence, yet you have almost daily mass shootings that gun control could dramatically reduce. Not to mention that your armed forces operate in other countries pretty much at will. Your country is full of private anti-government militias. You're among the world's most violent peoples."

"Not all of us," Larry said. "But many are. My first clue came during the gold medal hockey game at the 1960 Olympics. An Eastern European coach was interviewed while the American and Russian teams warmed up.

"He said one team was fast, clever, and innovative and the other was rugged and intimidating. I remember thinking: those damned Russians better not try any rough stuff on us. But it turned out the Americans were the bruisers, and the Soviets were the guys with the admirable qualities."

"As I remember," Meier said, eyes twinkling, "you Americans won that game."

—∞—

In the madrasa the FBI had impounded and was searching, Larry asked for a progress report and was referred to Lanier Clark, the agent in charge.

"Any progress since yesterday?" he asked.

"We've been through this place twice," Clark replied. "Our last hope is the computers we took to our lab in case they're booby trapped. We've got our best man analyzing their contents."

—∞—

Workmen were remodeling the State Capitol Building's media room, forcing Larry to hold his press conference at the La Rivage Hotel. When his limousine arrived he opened his door before Darth Vader could and walked to the front door under an arched blue canopy.

Reporters stood three deep beside the path they'd left open for him. He ignored shouted questions.

Vader pretended to mop his brow with his handkerchief, making sure his face wouldn't appear in photographs. Normally he wore casual clothes. Today he was dressed to blend in with a roomful of men in suits and women in dresses.

From the podium, Larry voluntarily revealed that he'd brought in—and recently relieved—Moshe Meier. That, he'd decided, was preferable to having his opponents do it when they inevitably discovered that Meier had been involved in widespread wiretaps without warrants.

As a result, tonight's news broadcasters would open their programs interviewing civil libertarians who'd point out the dangers inherent in such activities by the government.

Opponents of having the Guard in South Central—Avery King chief among them—would miss no opportunity to insult Meier and his men as hired guns, though they hadn't been paid or fired a single shot.

Some people would accept Larry's apology at face value, but others would criticize him until the headlines changed.

This was a gamble that could make or break him.

The package marked Extremely Urgent had been sent by FBI agent Lanier Clark.

While Larry signed for it, the delivery man said, "I admire what you're doing. Bringing in that Israeli was a smart move—no matter what the damn Democrats say. In my book, you're the best governor we've ever had."

Grinning, Larry told him, "Be sure to tell your friends."

Larry opened the box in his private office and found a sheaf of pages and a note.

'When I searched that Muslim school's computer,' it read, 'I found this diary. It details the help Muhammad Nasheed revealed from Iran and is so revealing that the computer was rigged to explode if anyone tried to access it without the password.'

Larry thumbed through the pages, surprised to see Emily's name on one. When he joined her in the living room, she was in the midst of a huge yawn.

"Who was at the door?" she asked.

"A delivery man. No big deal."

"In that case why the Extremely Urgent label?"

"I won't know until I read it, and that could take hours. Why don't you go to bed? I'll fill you in tomorrow."

"After years of marriage, you should know that I don't like being protected and prefer to be told the truth no matter how unpleasant."

"It's a copy of a diary the FBI found in a computer from that *madrasa* they've been searching."

"May I read it with you?" she asked. "You can pass me the pages as you finish them."

Every time he finished a page, Larry handed it to Emily. Soon she'd caught up and was standing behind him, reading over his shoulder. Then she jumped ahead and finished before he did.

When Larry was done, Emily asked, "Do you think the writer really did what he claims to have done?"

"How else would he know details the police kept secret?"

"What's on that page you didn't show me?"

"Whoever wrote this is planning to rape and kill you." Larry handed her a page he'd slipped under the couch.

—ɱ—

When Governor Webster left the hospital during Larry's La Rivage press conference, he'd looked well enough to resume his duties. At his own press conference later that day, he generated headlines by urging California's legislature to pass a resolution demanding Larry withdraw the Guard.

"He must not be ready to resume his duties," Larry told Ted Roffman at their morning meeting. "He wouldn't call for a legislative resolution if he could simply resume his duties and withdraw the Guard himself."

"Don't count on it," Ted cautioned. "Webster's a consummate politician and not averse to having others do his dirty work."

Later that day, Brian Pickering, Webster's Chief of Staff, called Ted and invited Larry to lunch.

"The Governor," Pickering explained, "wants to arrange a smooth transfer of power back to himself."

That afternoon, Darth Vader drove Larry and Ted to a restaurant popular among Sacramento politicians. When they arrived, Webster and Pickering were waiting at a table with two empty chairs. Pickering stood while Ted and Larry seated themselves.

Webster remained sitting and launched some pre-lunch small talk, punctuated with flashes of his made-for-television smile. When the waiter brought their food, he got down to business.

"From the start," he began, "I've been opposed to having the Guard in South Central. It smacks of racism."

"According to your use of the word," Roffman said, "a racist is anyone who doesn't judge Blacks by a less stringent standard than he uses for everyone else."

"The National Guard would never engage in shootouts in White neighborhoods," Webster said, "which proves—"

"There are no comparable threats in White neighborhoods," Roffman interrupted.

"That's enough, Ted," Larry broke in. "You both remind me of a quote attributed to Emily West: "There's no such thing as conversation. There are intersecting monologues, that's all."

After their meeting with Governor Webster, Darth Vader drove Larry and Ted several blocks before either spoke.

"Webster wants us to believe he'll resume his duties soon," Roffman broke the silence, "but I think he and Pickering were hiding his real condition. He never took a step while we were watching, and he let Pickering do most of the talking."

"Don't underestimate him," Larry told Ted. "He's a formidable politician with thirty-six years experience."

"That puts you ahead of him," Roffman said. "He hasn't had thirty-six years of experience. He's had one year of experience thirty-six times."

No one at the Los Angeles Police Department could remember a similar breakthrough. The diary Lanier Clark had found contained names, places, and dates, and revealed that a series of seemingly random events had been a well-planned, well-financed conspiracy.

It also gave them a trail to follow while attempting to establish the writer's identity.

CHAPTER FORTY-ONE
HOWARD DOANES

THAT AFTERNOON Howard Doanes, Speaker of the California Assembly, called Ted Roffman and scheduled a meeting with Larry.

"He's probably getting ready to help Webster discredit you," Ted told Larry. "You're the likely Republican candidate in next year's gubernatorial election. The Democrats would love to hand you another humiliating setback on the heels of the Moshe Meier scandal."

"Doanes seemed sincere back when he first offered to help me," Larry replied. "I'll keep my guard up, but I'm going to give him the benefit of the doubt."

Doanes arrived in a relaxed, jovial mood, making Larry all the more curious to see what was coming. Or more precisely, from what direction it would come.

"My offer," the Speaker began, "to show you the political ropes is still good. Are you ready to climb into the ring."

"I've been in the ring for months," Larry said.

"That's par for the course. Politics move slowly. You invest your time and wait for results, sometimes in vain." Doanes paused. "I understand you met with Governor Webster yesterday."

"Yes. He says he'll be back on the job soon."

"He won't, and he knows it. He's putting you off balance. You have at least a few months, unless the legislature cuts off CANG's funding."

"What are the chances of that?" Larry asked.

"It's definitely possible, despite my opposition. I was disappointed when you didn't contact me to work out a deal on funding your Y.P.P job training program."

"I had enough money from private sources," Larry said, "and thought it best to go to you after you'd had a chance to see it in action. At the moment we have a thousand young men and women being trained for good jobs."

"A thousand is a drop in the bucket. Only the government can finance a program big enough to do any real good. Will you be running for governor in the next election?"

"No matter what I say, it could be the wrong answer."

"You strike me as a man who tells the truth or doesn't say anything."

"I can't imagine any circumstances that would make me run for office again."

"Good. You'll accomplish more if you aren't concerned about how your actions look to voters, the media, or anyone else. That gives you an advantage over most politicians." Doanes' eyes searched Larry's face before he continued. "Governor Webster wants the legislature to force the Guard out of South Central. The votes are there. That's why I'm here."

"To ask me to withdraw the Guard voluntarily?" Larry asked.

"Hardly," Doanes returned. "I want you to help me delay and change the outcome of that vote. Here's what I have in mind."

Later Larry faxed a copy of Muhammad Nasheed's diary to Winston Baker, the man who'd authored RAND Corporation's study predicting a catastrophic riot in South Central. A day later, Baker called Larry.

"I don't know how this diary affected you," Baker began, "but it scared me spitless. Blacks worldwide revere Toussaint L'Ouverture because he led an army of slaves in a successful revolt that freed tens of thousands of slaves in Haiti and the Dominican Republic.

"The author of this diary, however, worships Toussaint—not because he freed slaves—but because his men killed thousands of Caucasians. He wants to emulate Toussaint and go much farther."

"He's got a good start," Larry said, "after engineering the Tourist Murders … stirring up the mob that destroyed much of South Central … murdering Carl Young, Gene Rice, and Tony Jackson … and training a private army that has killed hundreds of guardsmen and LAPD officers."

"He aspires to go much further with the help of a huge audience conveniently provided by our country's indulgences in slavery and segregation."

"How can we deprive him of that audience?" Larry asked.

"Start by publicizing his diary. People are more difficult to manipulate when they know who's doing it and why."

Howard Doanes had never brought a bill up for a vote that failed to pass it, and he wasn't about to spoil that record.

"The Legislature," he told Larry during their latest phone call, "is oh, so close to passing your Y.P.P. funding package. The Senate is ready to approve it, but I'm several votes short in the Assembly. Could Emily give us a hand with that?"

"I'll broach the subject tonight," Larry replied.

More than willing to help, Emily suggested forming groups to lobby Assembly members who were opposed or undecided. In a matter of hours she had volunteers for five groups, and the following morning they gathered in Larry's office to prepare talking points.

At the lectern, Emily adjusted the microphone and said, "Each of you is free to select his or her talking points. I've invited some speakers to help."

The first was Winston Baker from the RAND Corporation. He read selections from Muhammad Nasheed's diary.

Next was a boy who'd left a gang in order to join a Y.P.P. job training program and now did high-paying construction work on weekends and during summer vacation.

Then they heard from the teenage son of a single mother. Hours after promising her he'd leave his gang, he'd watched her die after being hit by a bullet intended for him.

Several speakers later, Emily introduced Stephen Curry, the Golden State Warriors' retired legend whose long-range shooting had changed basketball.

"Aspiring to play a professional sport can bring substantial benefits, even for those who don't make the big time," Curry said in conclusion. "They can lower their sights and play in semi professional leagues. They can give up their dreams and play for fun. Or they can pursue another career using the important lessons sports teach."

Four days later, Doanes called Emily with good news.

"The Assembly," he began, "rewrote the Y.P.P. funding bill to include everything I requested plus an additional eight million to expand the job program."

—~—

Muhammad Nasheed sat slumped in a small room with the shades drawn, head in hands. He was on the run and his top lieutenants were dead or jailed. After several thrashings from the National Guard in White neighborhoods, the Federation of Gangs' appetite for revolution was wavering.

His attempts to recruit from gangs in Oakland, Chicago, and New York were producing few results. And that morning his most-trusted right-hand man had given reporter Brian Waterman a six-inch headline:

'Muhammad Nasheed's birth name was Jamal King.'

—~—

Shortly after marrying at one of Sacramento's Baptist Churches, Michael Bridges and Regina Bradley left for a ten-day honeymoon in Hawaii.

When Bridges returned to work and walked into the governor's office, Larry was at his desk, reading *Black War Heroes* by Lewis Franklin. He closed it, marking his place with an index card.

"You look good," he told Michael. "You must have enjoyed your honeymoon."

"Every second of it," Michael replied. "Can we discuss my report on the Young People's Project?"

"Your timing's perfect." Larry opened a folder. "I just read it."

"I hope you approve of my changes in Tony's policies?"

"I didn't put you in that job so I could tell you what to do," Larry teased. "I knew you'd make good decisions."

"Most of the changes are minor," Bridges said. "Before I took over, field trips and other rewards went to the kids with the best grades. Now students can also qualify by handing in extra credit work."

"How do you enforce your new dress code?"

"I don't have to. Peer pressure does it for me."

"Your report," Larry said, "didn't say much about your Sexual Counseling Center."

"It provides pregnant girls with no-cost parenting classes, vitamins, and prenatal care. It also offers sexually active kids tests for Sexually Transmitted Diseases as well as antibiotics, condoms, and counseling. Since the riot, the Guard took over those services, but there's a long waiting list.

"We also have a program for disruptive students the schools removed from regular classrooms. It's voluntary and offers vocational and on-the-job training for careers of their choosing."

—∾—

Howard Doanes answered the door to his San Francisco-style Victorian bungalow.

"Come in," he greeted Larry and Darth Vader.

Dressed in a bathrobe and carrying a folded newspaper under his arm, he led the way to his dining room. There he sat at the head of the table while his wife served eggs, ham slices, country-fried potatoes, and toast.

Then he pointed to the patio and suggested to Vader, "If you take your breakfast outside, you'll enjoy a spectacular view and a cool breeze."

When he and Larry were alone, he used his last half-slice of toast to mop the remaining egg yolk from his plate and slide it into his large, loose mouth.

"I had to call in a lot of favors," he told Larry, "but I have the votes to table Governor Webster's resolution calling upon the President to withdraw the National Guard from South Central."

"Enlighten me," Larry said. "Why'd you do that? You're a states right's advocate and don't like having the Guard in South Central any more than Governor Webster and President Ripley do."

"Unfortunately the end sometimes justifies the means," Doanes replied. "If the president and Congress hadn't usurped powers not granted by the Constitution, most Blacks would still be educated in inferior segregated schools and prevented from voting.

"I'm sorry they were once slaves, but it's time for them to get over it. Lots of other races have suffered the same fate. Fortunately that's behind us, but Blacks weren't the only or even the first race to suffer mass oppression.

"In the Middle Ages serfs in Europe and Russia were tied to the land and were sold right along with it. For centuries Circassian women from Europe's Caucus Mountains were forced into harems in the Middle East and Africa.

"In Egypt, Hebrews were enslaved for somewhere between two and four hundred years. As enlightened as ancient Greeks were, they brought slaves from a host of countries.

"Tens of thousands of aboriginal people were kidnapped from Polynesia and other South Pacific islands and forced to labor in Peru.

"The list goes on and on."

CHAPTER FORTY-TWO
THE SAFE HOUSE

ON NEW Year's Eve, the dining room table had been extended. Its Queen Anne chairs were full when Emily served dinner. Less than a month before the scheduled birth of the child she and Larry were adopting, that event dominated the conversation.

The doorbell rang three times in less than a minute. Sighing, Larry answered it and saw Lanier Clark, the FBI agent, on the porch.

"Happy New Year," Larry greeted. "Please come in."

"Not right now, Governor," Clark said abruptly. "We believe the gangs are planning something big this evening. As a precaution, we have men guarding your house and units patrolling the neighborhood."

Across the street, a woman waited for her dog to finish sniffing a fire hydrant. A man in jeans and sweatshirt walked up and flashed a badge, then checked her driver's license before thanking her.

"This is secure," Clark told Larry, handing him a two-way radio. "You can reach me by pressing this button. I won't be far away. And as an added precaution, I brought a friend of yours."

Larry saw Darth Vader coming up his porch's long staircase. Clark hurried away. Looking worried, Vader quickly closed and locked the door.

"Take this seriously," he told Larry as he began shutting curtains. "Stay away from windows, and let me answer the door."

"If we're spending the night together," Larry teased, "you should at least tell me your real name. Emily thinks it must be something like Throckmorton B. Thimblebottom or Yancy Thadwick Lipschitz."

—~—

"Do you mind if I switch to another channel?" Larry asked late that night when CNN's news had become repetitive.

"Suit yourself," Vader said, trimming his fingernails.

"Why do you do that so often?" Larry asked.

"So my nails won't interfere if I have to use my gun."

Lanier Clark's two-way radio buzzed.

"I'm on my way to your front door," Clark said. "We're taking you and your wife to a safe house."

—~—

As Clark's car sped down deserted streets, he told Larry, "A group of men destroyed a Metropolitan Transit Authority bus, killing forty-one people. LAPD is withholding all other information while they identify the victims and notify their next-of-kin."

The television in the safe house was on, and a news anchorman was broadcasting an update. The attackers had used rocket propelled grenades and the only survivor—a six-year-old-girl—had died in an ambulance on the way to a hospital.

With forty-one deaths on his conscience, Larry couldn't help regretting his decision to send Moshe Meier back to Israel. He'd made a terrible mistake.

—∾—

Watching television the next day, Larry gradually learned more about the attack. The media had named it The Westwood Bus Massacre. Jamal King was a prime suspect, and a hundred-thousand-dollar reward had been offered for information leading to his arrest.

When Lanier Clark stopped by that afternoon, Larry asked, "Do you have any leads?"

"One, but it's flimsy," Clark replied. "A man matching his description was seen boarding a flight to Iran. The authorities there have been their usual cooperative selves, of course."

"How long are you planning to keep us here?" Larry asked.

"Until Jamal King is no longer a threat," Clark replied.

"Will it help if I volunteer to be a target?"

"The FBI doesn't use human beings for bait."

"Maybe you should in this case."

CHAPTER FORTY-THREE
A PERSON WHO DIDN'T EXIST YESTERDAY

AN ORDINARY morning became a sweet memory for Emily as Darth Vader drove her and Larry to work.

"South Central has been calm for over a month," Larry said, "and nothing has been heard from Jamal King. The FBI believes he may have killed himself. If you're ready to move ahead with our personal plans, I am as well. The adoption agency has an available newborn girl—still in the hospital—and we're first in line."

She slid closer to him as he continued, "The birth mother has signed adoption papers. I was so excited I forgot to get more details."

"What race is she?" Emily asked.

"I didn't ask and don't care. The important thing is she's healthy."

"I'm happy for you both," Darth Vader said as he turned into their driveway.

As soon as they got to their bedroom, Larry sensed that his wife was in the mood to make love. Emily didn't take off her skirt and blouse in the bathroom, as usual. She faced away and slowly revealed a tapered back that widened into a shapely, feminine bottom.

She'd never considered herself beautiful, and now she was showing her age.

She turned, surprised to see Larry responding to the view. He put his arms around her and pulled her close. Her moist pubic hair brushed against him.

"I'm glad you don't shave there," he said. "You're more arousing when natural."

He reached over, pulled the comforter from their bed, and laid Emily down. Her golden tan stood out against the ivory sheet. She turned away, and he snuggled up behind her, lavishing kisses on her neck and running his fingertips along protruding shoulder blades.

When Emily faced him, her sensitive nipples were swollen and darker. With her wide-open mouth pressed to his, she probed his mouth with her tongue.

Taking her in his arms, Larry rolled onto his back. He liked having her on top facing him, and she liked being there.

Holding Emily's hips, Larry aligned their bodies and slowly pushed inside. Her gray-blue eyes were alive with desire.

All the way inside now, he moved slowly, stimulating her sensitive spot. She flushed bright red. Her breathing became deeper, more rapid. As he built up speed, he heard that familiar whimper deep in her throat. Then her thighs tightened and her body went rigid.

He'd waited as long as he could.

—ᨓ—

Afterward, they fell asleep, still in each other's arms.

Later Larry woke with the nagging feeling something important was about to happen. Slowly—as if through a fog—it came to him. He and Emily were picking up their new daughter that afternoon.

Turning his head, he saw Emily—fully dressed—come through the bedroom door with two glasses of cranberry juice.

She handed him one, then said, "I laid out your clothes. Darth Vader said the drive to Mercy General Hospital should take about thirty minutes."

Emily and Larry were at the hospital's nursery window admiring the babies, especially their new daughter. When feeding time was over, a nurse took them to a private room, then brought the girl they'd been watching.

"What did you name her?" she asked Emily.

"We named her Taylor," Emily replied. "Well, *I* named her Taylor."

"Taylor seems to be in perfect health," the nurse said. "You can take her home with you as soon as the doctor gives her a final check up. The sooner you take over her care, the sooner she'll start bonding with you, which is especially important in interracial adoptions."

"It's hard to believe," Emily told Larry when they were alone, "that a person who didn't exist yesterday is coming to live with us today."

"I'm one of your many fans, Governor," the security guard said as Larry, Emily, and Taylor left the hospital. "You'll get my vote from now on."

"I appreciate that," Larry said, stopping, "but I'm quitting while I'm ahead."

"That's a shame. You're the best governor California ever had."

Parked in a loading zone, Darth Vader got out of the governor's limousine and waved.

"Jamal King finally surfaced," he said with urgency. "LAPD's Chief Johnson needs you ... now. I ordered Emily another driver. He'll be here soon. Emily and the baby can wait in the lobby."

Speeding away from the hospital, Vader told Larry, "Chief Johnson set up a Command Center near West Florence Avenue and South Western Avenue. Jamal King hijacked a school bus full of kids and took them to the Southern California Schoolbook Depository. The police have him surrounded. That's all I know at the moment."

—∿—

Before the Carl Young Riot, the vehicle housing LAPD's portable Command Center bore LAPD logos. During the Carl Young Riot, when police became a prime target for gangs, it was repainted to resemble a delivery van.

As the governor's limousine screeched to a stop, Chief Johnson opened the Command Center's door and looked outside.

"Is King still in the Schoolbook Depository?" Larry asked.

"We think so," Johnson replied, waving Larry inside. "The Department of Building and Safety sent us the building's blueprints, and we know there are no underground passageways leading to other locations."

A thunderous explosion rocked the Command Center. On the viewing screen showing the Depository's closest side, Larry saw an old brick building, a chunk missing from a corner, three stories up. A column of coal-black smoke boiled through the opening and rose toward the sky.

"Another of King's demonstrations," Johnson growled. "He wants to make sure we believe he's got C-4 planted throughout the building, including where the kids are."

"How many men are you up against?"

"We have no idea, but it doesn't matter. With all those kids in there, we don't dare go in."

On another viewing screen Larry saw a school bus parked at the Depository's entrance. Through a window he saw squad cars, their dome lights flashing, uniformed officers crouched behind their engines for protection.

"You're here," the Chief said, "because King told our regular hostage negotiator he won't deal with anyone but you."

News of the standoff traveled fast. After a news flash interrupted *The Oprah Winfrey Show*, Emily switched to CNN, where Wolf Blitzer's daughter was giving her audience the known details.

She dialed Larry's cell phone number. When it rang, he hurried from Chief Johnson's Command Center and answered outside.

"Sorry for the delay," he said. "Something unexpected came up."

"I'm watching your 'something unexpected' on television," she said.

"There's no need to worry. King can't hurt me over the telephone, and that's as close as I'll get to him. You have my word."

"I'm taking that as an ironclad promise," Emily said. "When this is over, I want you back, alive and well. Please."

Back inside Chief Johnson's Command Center, Larry was briefed by the hostage negotiator, Ken Richards.

"I've never been up against a hostage taker I didn't think I could wear down," Richards said, shaking his head. "Most criminals use hostages for defense. But this guy is looking forward to killing his and probably himself as well.

"I'll get him on the line. Whatever else you do, make it crystal clear you're not going inside that building. Period."

Richards dialed his cell phone, listened, and hung up without speaking.

"King won't talk until he can see you," Richards told Larry. "Anyone got an idea how we can make that happen without risk to the Governor?"

"I saw some stand-alone, full-length mirrors in a nearby clothing store," one of the officers said. "We could put one around a corner from the Governor."

"That's worth a try," Richards said.

After the mirror was in position, Larry and Richards walked toward the corner from which it faced the School-book Depository. When his image completely filled the mirror, Larry stopped and Richards remained out of sight.

Larry dialed the number Richards had given him.

"I hope this is Governor Winslow," an eerily calm voice answered. "To show this isn't some sort of high tech trick, follow my instructions, quickly. Raise your right hand... stand on your left leg only... turn around, counterclockwise... pat your stomach.

"Good, but if we're going to do business, it has to be face-to-face."

"That's absolutely out of the question," Larry said firmly. "I'm here to arrange for—"

"You'll come in here eventually," the voice interrupted, its tone still placid. "Why don't you do it before I start killing kids?"

"I'm willing to give you guarantees that aren't normally offered in situations like this," Larry persisted. "If you'll release half the children you're holding—"

"To show my sincerity," King interrupted, "I'll send one hostage with a message for you. His name is Bobby Samuels, and he's from Beverly Hills. I want your answer in ten minutes or less."

"Hold your fire," Ken Richards said into a transmitter. "They're sending a hostage out."

From Richard's transmitter, Larry heard the SWAT team leader instruct his snipers, "Make sure this kid isn't rigged with explosives."

Then Richards told Larry, "You did well. Getting one of those kids freed is a promising start."

A White boy appeared in the Depository's entrance and started toward the mirror. Slowly and self-consciously, he stepped into the street.

Bobby was halfway across the street, lower lip between his teeth. When he was three feet from safety he was slammed forward and blood seemed to explode from his chest. Falling forward, he looked down. The horror on his face said he'd lived long enough to know what happened.

"My God!" Larry exclaimed. "Why?"

"Did you get my message?" the familiar voice asked, chillingly dispassionate.

Larry's throat constricted. "Yes."

"I still have forty-two kids in here. I'll kill all but five unless you become a hostage in their places."

"You win," Larry said, "but I need some assurances."

"These are the best you'll get. I'll release half the hostages. When I can no longer see them, I'll let ten more go. When they're halfway across the street, you step out in plain sight and walk to the Depository. If you don't, my men will machine gun the kids."

CHAPTER FORTY-FOUR
BIGGER ISN'T NECESSARILY BETTER

COMING OUT of the Command Center, Darth Vader begged Larry, "Don't go in that building. If you do, you're a dead man."

"As long as there's the slightest chance of success, I'm going," Larry declared.

"In that case, you may as well go down fighting." Vader reached behind his lapel and pulled out a .357 Magnum revolver. "The best thing about these is that if you hit your target, he stops then and there. Problem is, you can't conceal them on your person. Luckily for you, I have a weapon you may not have to hide."

He reached inside his shoe and took out what appeared to be a cell phone.

"The latest in terrorist weaponry," Vader said. "They don't attract attention and fire a small caliber bullet that's reasonably accurate at short distances. Their weakness is that your victim sometimes dies slowly because the bullet has to be perfectly placed for a kill."

He leaned a small sandbag against a nearby concrete wall.

"Fire away," he said. "Don't worry—those small bullets won't be heard inside the Schoolbook Depository."

Larry took four practice shots, missing with the first two. Then he scored two hits.

"Aim for the head," Vader advised, "and don't miss. This thing holds only four bullets. It can, however, be quickly reloaded."

He demonstrated.

—∞—

A national television audience watched as Larry Winslow and twenty children crossed Western Avenue in opposite directions. The view was from a helicopter above. Twenty LAPD officers dashed into the street. Each picked up a child, shielded him or her, and dashed to safety.

Larry was halfway across the street, and the camera was aimed at him. He had a cellphone pressed to his ear.

Fearing her husband would be shot dead at any moment, Emily shuddered as Jamal King reeled him in.

"Please God," she whispered, kissing Taylor as the baby hungrily nursed. "Bring him back to us no worse for wear."

—∞—

The lights were off in the Schoolbook Depository lobby. When Larry's eyes adjusted, he saw a green flashing light on a nearby closed-circuit television camera. Somewhere, Jamal King was watching him on a monitor.

The voice on Larry's cell phone instructed him to take the freight elevator to the second floor, a cavernous room where lift trucks had stacked crates of furniture when the building housed a moving and storage company. Now it contained shelves loaded with cartons of school books.

Sitting on the floor—wearing backpacks, presumably filled with C-4 explosive—terrified children watched Larry come out of the elevator. He saw guards with rocket propelled grenades and counted twenty hostages.

"Stay where you are," a guard ordered, "while I make sure no one else is coming."

Later—satisfied that Larry was alone—the man spoke again, "Take the elevator to the top floor."

On the seventh floor two giant hands grabbed Larry as he left the elevator, then slammed him against the wall, hammering the air from his lungs.

"Empty your pockets," the man said, "and take off your belt and shoes."

The man scanned Larry with an electronic wand and frisked him, far less gently and discreetly than an airport screener would have. In the room's faint light he looked huge.

"May I ask ... " Larry began.

"Shut the fuck up," the man barked, unaware that what he was searching for was in Larry's hand.

By the time the man finished his search, he was going through the motions. Convinced he wouldn't find anything, he didn't. Satisfied, he took Larry to another room.

Larry recognized the man inside, even though they'd never met. He resembled his father physically. But having dedicated his life to spreading what he considered the only true faith, his manner, clothing, and grooming were low-key—typical of Muslim fanatics.

From where King stood, he could watch approaches to the building, some through shuttered windows, others on closed circuit monitors. More monitors showed him what was happening in other parts of the building. If SWAT teams came, he'd know long before they found him.

Behind him, crates of rocket propelled grenades guaranteed that—if attacked—he and his men wouldn't kill their enemies one at a time.

"Welcome," King said. "My faith obliges me to extend hospitality to guests, which is what you are since you're here at my invitation."

"If shooting that boy was a sample of your hospitality," Larry said, "I'll gladly forgo my share. Why am I here?"

"You'll find out soon enough." King's smile peeled his lips away from poorly cared-for teeth and gums. "When you came here today, you were determined not to come inside this building, right? But here you are. You have no idea what I can do, but you'll soon see."

Larry's weapon could be taken from him at any second, even if not recognized for what it was. But to use it with any chance of success, he needed King and his bodyguard to be in the same vicinity so he could shoot both without losing time acquiring his second target.

"The police," Larry said, "have you surrounded. They've got snipers with night vision goggles...jamming equipment to disable the Depository's video monitoring system... and sensors that can see through these walls. How can you possibly get out of here?"

"Courtesy of the National Guard which has promised me a Bradley armored personnel carrier." King glanced at his watch. "It'll be here soon, Omar. Time for the head harness."

Larry leaned over and slipped the cell phone pistol inside his shoe while pretending to tie the laces.

Omar kicked his legs out from under him.

"Sit up," he growled, then slipped a web-like contraption made of nylon straps over Larry's head and fastened its chin buckle. The straps dangling from its left side swung wildly when Omar grabbed Larry's arm and hurried him across the room to the freight elevator.

There Omar attached the head-harness' hanging straps to a sawed-off shotgun, securing its barrel inches from Larry's ear. If the gun was fired, his would be a closed-casket funeral. The shell's pellets would be tightly grouped when they took his head off.

"My finger's on the trigger," Omar warned. "If you pull, I pull."

When the elevator door opened on the second floor the man guarding the hostages was waiting.

"Kill the hostages after we leave," Omar told him. "Then meet us at the rendezvous point."

CHAPTER FORTY-FIVE
STRANGER AND STRANGER

DARTH VADER was worried. Why had Larry been out of touch for so long? After a lifetime of being told not to hurt people, had he lost his nerve? Had King recognized the cell phone for what it really was? There were many possibilities. The man he'd protected for months wasn't necessarily dead.

From the governor's limousine, Vader and hostage negotiator Ken Richards saw lights go on in the Depository's lobby. Its entrance was designed for colder climates. Two parallel rows of glass doors were separated by a foyer, reducing the amount of air that came in with foot traffic.

As close as possible to the Depository's entrance, the Bradley's rear entry ramp had been lowered. To reach it, hostages, terrorists, and Larry—if he was alive—would have to walk unprotected across an open area.

Then Vader saw a massive man steering Larry Winslow into the Depository's foyer. A shotgun attached to a head harness pointed at Larry's temple.

"Any idea what that contraption is?' Richards asked as one of the terrorists rolled a line of male mannequins into view. They were on wheels, connected by metal rods, and draped with tarps that were inches from the ground on three sides and folded up on the other.

"Could be a way of getting King and his men from the Depository to the Bradley," Vader said.

"This is getting stranger and stranger. What next?"

They didn't have to wait long for an answer.

—∾—

In the Schoolbook Depository's foyer, a line of chained-together hostages were padlocked, one to each mannequin. Then King, Omar, and Larry joined them, and the remaining tarp was lowered, depriving police snipers of visible targets.

By then it was dark and LAPD's portable spotlights were turned on.

—∾—

Inside the overcrowded Bradley, Omar slammed Larry to the floor and detached the shotgun from his head harness. Then he and Jamal King shoehorned themselves into the operators' seats and studied the instrument panel.

"They've made changes in these since I last drove one," King said, "but nothing major."

Larry heard the engine start and smelled diesel smoke.

While King's and Omar's attention was elsewhere, Larry pulled his heels against his butt and slid his cuffed hands under his feet. While taking the cell phone from his shoe he lost his grip and it clattered on the floor.

The Bradley's engine was loud. Neither King nor Omar had heard. King's assault rifle lay on the floor, more than an arm's length from him. Omar's shorter, more maneuverable sawed-off shotgun was across his lap, making him the more dangerous of the two.

Larry took a deep breath. The handcuffs hindered him as he picked up the cell phone pistol, then pointed and steadied it with both hands, aiming for Omar's head, a few feet away.

He pushed numbers one and two on the keypad and heard the sound of bullets smashing through bone.

As King reached for his rifle, Larry pressed three and four on the keypad, placing two bullets three inches apart, in King's cheek and jaw. Blinking and gasping, King fell back against the control panel.

Larry reloaded and checked each man for a pulse, finding none. Then the now-driverless Bradley hit something solid and stopped. He turned the engine off.

A foul stench overpowered the sour smell of gunpowder. After dying, Jamal King had lost control of his bowels.

When Darth Vader opened the Bradley's rear access, fresh air poured through the opening.

"I can't tell you," he told Larry, "how glad I am to see you."

"Not nearly as glad as I am to be here," Larry replied. "This is no place for children. Let's get them out of here."

Outside, Larry saw the blood splattered on several children. He took out his handkerchief and tenderly cleaned their faces and arms, as if that would also purge what had happened from their minds.

"Can you please help get these kids away from the building?" Larry asked a Sergeant who was checking the Bradley's interior. "This isn't over. The men still in the building are going to blow it up."

"With any luck," the Sergeant said grimly, "we're ahead of them this time."

Blocks away, a Guardsman with bolt cutters removed Larry's handcuffs. Nearby, female police officers and a lady from Child Protective Services were re-uniting hostages with their worried parents.

A small girl was wrapped in her mother's arms. Her mom was whispering soothing words. Periodically, the girl leaned back and described what had happened. Between installments, she snuggled close, seeking the comfort of another hug.

"Where's Bobby Samuels?" the girl asked. "Those men said they were going to let him go. Is he okay?"

Larry tore himself away. Someone else could answer that uncomfortable question. He walked over to a boy sitting alone on a curb, chin cupped in his hands.

"What's your name?" he asked.

"Lavon Johnson," the boy said.

"Aren't your mom and dad here yet, Lavon?"

"They ain't coming.'"

"Maybe they got delayed in traffic."

"Naw. My mom don't come home lotsa nights, and her boyfriend don't give a shit about me."

"I'll take you home," Larry offered. "On the way we'll get a hamburger or a hot dog. Would you like that?"

"Yeah. If you keep your promise. My mom—"

"I appreciate your good intentions, Governor Winslow," the lady from Child Protective Services interrupted, "but I'll take this boy home. I want to evaluate his situation before he gets put back into it."

The next face Larry saw was the last one he wanted to see. With an effort he met Avery King's eyes.

"Did you have to kill my son?" Avery asked.

"I had no choice," Larry replied.

From behind, Darth Vader grabbed King's shoulders, and steered him away.

"The way I see it, Avery," Larry heard Vader say, "you helped kill your boy by filling him full of hatred."

Larry was exhausted. No matter how casually movie heroes shot villains... no matter how unavoidable killing might be... it affected the person who took life as well as the one who lost it.

"Emily flew into LAX," Vader said, watching to make sure King kept going. "The Highway Patrol picked her up and is bringing her here."

Larry looked down at his bloody arms, shirt, and pants.

"You can spruce up in the Command Center," Vader suggested.

"What happened to the hostages and Jamal King's men who stayed behind in the Depository?" Larry asked.

"They tried to escape through a little-known tunnel left over from the days of prohibition and bootlegging. But LAPD also knew about it and was waiting for them. When push came to shove, they didn't blow up the building. Police are bringing out the rest of the hostages and removing the explosives, floor by floor."

After Larry's sponge bath he and Darth Vader stood talking on the curb in front of the Command Center. A Highway Patrol car stopped at the curb. Carrying Taylor, Emily got out and handed her baby to Vader. Wrapping both arms around Larry, she lay her head against his chest.

"I'm glad I realized how much I love you while you're still alive," she told him, squeezing tighter.

Larry bent down and gave her a long kiss.

Vader looked away, allowing them the closest thing to privacy they'd have for the rest of that eventful evening.

EPILOGUE

THE DAY before leaving office, Larry gave his final speech as governor. It was broadcast nationally and watched by a record number of viewers.

"Despite their treatment in America," he began, "her Blacks have defended her every time she's been threatened. One of the first men shot by the British during the Boston Massacre was a Negro, Crispus Attucks.

"During the subsequent Revolutionary War, 5,000 of America's Blacks fought alongside her Whites at the battles of Concord and Bunker Hill.

"After initially refusing to allow Negroes in his Continental Army, George Washington accepted five all-Black units. These included a regiment that repulsed three furious British charges which threatened to turn the American flank at the Battle of Rhode Island.

"During the War of 1812, roughly ten percent of the sailors in America's navy were Black, and the commander of the USS *Constitution* said he'd never seen better fighters.

"An example of their courage was provided by John Davis, a Black sailor aboard the *Governor Tompkins* who had both legs torn off by a British cannon ball. As the battle raged on, he lay on the deck begging crew members to throw him overboard so he wouldn't be in their way.

"At the Battle of New Orleans, slaves and freedmen helped General Andrew Jackson's army defeat a British force that outnumbered it two-to-one.

"Early in the American Civil War, Robert Smalls and seven other sailors hijacked the Confederate gunboat, *Planter,* while its crew was ashore in Charleston, South Carolina.

"With Smalls wearing the Captain's uniform and imitating his walk, they sailed past Fort Sumter's cannons at the mouth of the harbor and delivered *Planter* to the Union Navy.

"Nearly two hundred thousand Blacks voluntarily enlisted in the Union Army during our Civil War. Almost forty thousand were killed. At the Battle of New Market Heights, fourteen won Medals of Honor.

"Black Buffalo Soldiers won eighteen Medals of Honor during the Indian Wars and had by far the lowest desertion rate in the U.S. Army. During the Spanish-American War, the Buffalo Soldiers charged up San Juan Hill with Teddy Roosevelt's famed Rough Riders.

"When America entered World War I, French commanders were desperately short of men and New York's 369th Infantry was assigned to them. This all-Black regiment became known as the Harlem Hell Fighters.

"One of them, Private Henry Jackson, was wounded several times while single-handedly killing many of the twenty-four Germans who attacked his foxhole.

"The Harlem Hell Fighters spent more time on the front lines than any other American unit in that war. Often they were the only Allied troops between the Imperial German Army and Paris.

"At the Battle of Belleau Wood, they ignored an order to retreat, maintaining their record of never having lost ground to the enemy. And when a massive Allied offensive forced the Kaiser's troops to surrender, the 369th had fought its way closer to Germany than any other Allied outfit.

"During World War II, a million two hundred thousand Blacks served in America's armed forces. They were among the sailors who battled German submarines and fifty foot waves while their warships escorted merchantmen across the North Atlantic.

"They were among the Marines who fought their way ashore against fanatical Japanese resistance on Pacific Islands such as Iwo Jima. At the Battle of the Bulge, African American tank crews under George Patton earned a Presidential Unit Citation.

"Black fighter pilots, the Tuskegee Airmen—flying P-51 Mustang fighter planes with red tail fins—shot down more than a hundred enemy fighters while defending American bomber formations over Germany, earning the nickname 'Red-Tailed Angels.'

Heavyweight boxing champion, Joe Louis—an all-time great Black boxer—donated the purses from two of his title defenses to America's war effort.

"After seemingly endless American retreats at the beginning of the Korean War, an all-Black regiment gave us our first victory by taking the town of Yechon. Black troops served with distinction throughout that conflict as well as in Vietnam, Operation Desert Storm, Iraq, and Afghanistan.

"In the decades of the all-volunteer military, up to thirty percent of America's Army has been Black, even though they're only fourteen percent of our population.

"In 2020 after outgoing President Donald Trump lost his bid for reelection, an estimated eighty thousand of his White supporters gathered at the U.S. Capitol Building in Washington, D.C.

"Their goal was to prevent a joint session of Congress from certifying the victory of President-elect Joe Biden.

Encouraged by Trump to "fight like hell," more than two thousand fanatical Caucasian insurrectionists entered the Capitol building, some by force.

"The battle raged for hours. Several intruders died. Nearly two hundred police were injured, some seriously. Damage to the building totaled nearly three million dollars.

"The attack ultimately stalled, thanks to a thousand badly outnumbered Capitol policemen—almost forty percent of them Black. Risking their lives, these men helped preserve democracy in a nation that had treated their race badly for centuries.

"They were unsung heroes, and this nation is lucky to have had them."

Acknowledgements

The real Larry Winslow gave me my best job ever. I say *gave* because no one else would've hired me as a bank loan officer. But eventually, with Larry's help, I both succeeded and set aside enough money to pursue my dream career as an author.

I've never known anyone better at anything than Larry was at managing Tracy Federal Bank. His quick decisions gave bank examiners chills, but his competitors admired and envied him. Like me, they saw that he wasn't reckless. He simply thought faster than we did.

I named this novel's protagonist after him as a constant reminder of the character, personality, and competence I wanted to give him.

A heartfelt thank-you also goes to my test readers: Al Walker, Sherla Alberola, Ralph Albright, Mimi Busk-Downey, and, of course, the real Larry Winslow.

About the Author

VERNE R. ALBRIGHT grew up in the American West and at nineteen years of age took his first trip outside the United States... to Peru.

"I would have been a different person and lived a lesser life," he says, "if I'd never gone there. Peru was the first place where I felt completely at home, and I soon fell in love with its unique people."

Verne has since made sixty-five business trips to Peru.

"Finding a true calling is a miracle many people never experience," he says, "and Peru provided me with two. The first was Peruvian Paso horses, which I spent a half century promoting throughout the world. The second was Peru's fascinatingly rich history and culture, which provided material to feed a more-recently discovered passion—writing historical fiction, mostly set in Peru."

Albright lives in Calgary, Alberta, Canada, with his wife and five dogs.

Manufactured by Amazon.ca
Bolton, ON